Murder V

Alison Joseph

Chapter One

'Poison, you see,' Sylvia Ettridge said, positioning herself firmly in an armchair and folding her arms. 'That's why they thought it was a natural death to start with. And then of course it turns out that something nasty has been put in his night time cocoa.'

Agatha Christie sipped at her cup of tea and rather wished her neighbour would leave her in peace. Mrs. Ettridge always had a view on the plots she was writing, and, true, she was writing a poisoning, but there was no need for Sylvia to tell her what to do next.

'And of course, everyone at the vicarage is horrified.'

Agatha's annoyance went up a notch. Had she told her she was writing a poisoning at the vicarage? She had no memory of sharing her new story idea with anyone apart from her husband, and he never listened in any case.

'And what with the curate being my godson,' Mrs. Ettridge went on.

Now this was a step too far. The idea that she'd write Sylvia into the play … although, as she looked at her bossy neighbour, sitting on plump cushions in her voluminous turquoise dress and matching turban, Agatha thought it might not be such a bad idea.

Sunlight filtered through the curtains. The view beyond seemed peaceful, summery, the spire of the village church visible just above the hedgerows.

'So,' Sylvia was saying, 'I had to get involved. I went across there as soon as I heard, but it's crawling with police officers, they wouldn't even let me in to talk to Robert, I'll have to try again this afternoon.'

Agatha stared at her. 'Police?' she said.

'Well, yes, of course, after that poor young man was found dead at the vicarage, the vicar was bound to call the police, wasn't he?'

'But you said … poison?' she said, weakly.

'That's what they've been saying. I told you, initial reports suggest he was poisoned. Certainly not natural causes. But no sign of any injury, that's the point.'

Agatha got to her feet. 'Mrs. Ettridge, are you telling me that there has been a murder at the vicarage?'

Now it was Sylvia's turn to stare. 'Have you been listening to a word I've been saying? And surely you'd have heard the commotion. The poor boy was found this morning, dead, lying on the floor of the library there. Surely you heard all the motor cars, the dogs barking? Although, you are rather tucked away here. Anyway, I told poor Robert not to worry, and how you'd be just the person to talk to, what with your expertise in these matters, and so I've arranged to take you across there now, if that suits you, Mrs. Christie?'

'Robert?' Agatha picked up the tea pot, put it down again.

'The curate. My godson. Do try and concentrate. The dead boy is a chum of his from the clinic, Cecil Coates, he was just staying for a few days, and the awful thing is, while he was staying, this thing

5

happens. Robert's very upset, and it doesn't help that the Vicar was already a bit dubious about Robert's appointment, and this isn't going to help, is it?'

'Does Robert live at the vicarage too?'

Sylvia nodded. 'It's huge. The Vicar would just be rattling around there, with Eva the continental maid. The curate has a few rooms of his own, and that's where this awful thing happened.'

'And Robert's your godson?'

Sylvia's lips twitched with annoyance. 'Do try and listen, Mrs. Christie. He's the son of one of my oldest friends, Jean Sayer. When she married that man from Wellington, not our Wellington, unfortunately, the other one, and went off there to live, she entrusted me with his well-being. And now this. I'm going to look as if I really haven't been paying him sufficient attention. And her antipodean husband always had a dim view of me, this really isn't going to help. That's why he simply has to talk to you. Shall we go?'

'But – Sylvia...' Agatha tried to keep her voice level. 'It's simply out of the question.'

Mrs. Ettridge gazed at her in puzzlement. 'But – it's what you do.'

'Me?' Agatha stared at her, appalled. 'I write stories. I make things up. The idea that I might want to have anything to do with anything – real. I mean, that poor young man... I'm sorry, I can't possibly come with you.'

Mrs. Ettridge was staring at her, frowning. 'Oh, but you have to. I've told them all about you.'

'Well, you can un-tell them, then.' Agatha reached for her cup of tea, and sipped at it, even though it was cold.

There was a frosty silence. Then a ring at the doorbell, and a few moments later, a tousled woman in full riding costume was shown into the room.

'Agatha – you've simply got to help.'

'Mary – what on earth has happened?' Agatha looked at her friend, who was mud-spattered and tearful.

'I've come from the vicarage, we were just doing a gentle trot, Myrtle and I, and then suddenly there was a paper bag caught in the hedgerow, and you know how Myrtle hates anything flapping like that, so she was off, and I was riding out with Phoebe, you know her, Shirley Banks' daughter, and then both horses jumped the hedge into the vicar's field, and my horse is now cantering around the vicarage garden, terrified, poor love – she doesn't like religion any more than I do – and Phoebe's barely staying on, she's on Jimmie who's normally good as gold, but he's such a follower, and then it turns out there's been some awful commotion at the vicarage, apparently someone's been found dead, and the worse thing is it's some poor young man known to Phoebe, so I thought after we've rounded up the horses you can sit with Phoebe while these policeman talk to her and that way they'll be kind to her as you know all about policemen...' She stopped, breathless.

Agatha was aware of both women, waiting. Sylvia was still seated, slipping her gloves on, slowly, finger by finger. Mary was smoothing her hair back into its pins.

Agatha realized she had no choice.

'I'll tell Alice that I'll be half an hour,' she said.

Sylvia got to her feet. She nodded at Mary. 'So you know Shirley's girl. She must be pleased to have her daughter back from London. I gather Shirley's got Mr. Fullerton to keep an eye on her, keep her out of trouble. Isn't it funny how everyone knows everyone in this village?' She picked up her turquoise jacket and turned to Agatha. 'When we get there, have a chat with Robert, just the two of you, then he can speak in confidence. You can tell me everything he says tomorrow.'

Chapter Two

It occurred to Agatha that she'd never properly looked at the vicarage before. Of course, she'd always been aware of the large, red-brick building, the green tiling of the roof, the ornamental windows. But she'd never really noticed the overgrown garden, the uneven fencing, the damp around the sills.

The door was opened by a small, dark-haired woman, who gave a brief, unsmiling nod and ushered them inside.

'As I said,' Mrs. Ettridge said, in a loud whisper. 'Continental.'

A uniformed police constable appeared to be standing guard in the hallway. Then the vicar was coming towards them, his plump hand outstretched, his face round and pink above his dog collar.

'Mrs. Christie,' he said, in a rather wheezing voice.

'Reverend Collins,' she said, taking the proffered hand.

'I suppose you'll want to see the body, what with your line of work,' he said.

'Absolutely not,' she began to say, but he wasn't listening. His hand was warm and damp, and she let go as soon as was polite.

'Come along, come along,' he began to say, but then a policeman suddenly stepped forward, his arm outstretched. 'With all due respect, Sir, that is a crime scene in there. My orders are to let no one in.'

'But this is Mrs. Christie,' the vicar said, his indignation implying that all crime scenes should be accessible to one such as she.

'I'll check with my Sergeant outside,' the young constable said, and disappeared.

'The horses have calmed down,' the vicar was saying, turning to Mary. 'Your young friend seems to have found her nerve again.'

Mary went out to the field, leaving Agatha and Sylvia standing in the hall.

Behind the vicar there appeared a thin, awkward-looking young man with dark brown hair. Sylvia went to greet him.

'Robert, dear…'

He looked at her with apprehension. 'Mrs. Ettridge,' he said.

'Your mother sends her love and concern,' Mrs. Ettridge said to him. 'And do call me Auntie Sylvia.'

'How did Mother know?' He stared down at her, frowning.

'I told her, of course. I made a trunk telephone call.'

'I'd rather she hadn't heard,' he said to her.

'Oh, but –'

'What's done is done,' Robert said. 'Poor Cecil. It's just unfortunate he was here.'

There was a harsh set to his face, Agatha noticed, but just then the young policeman reappeared, and she was called away to the library, where another, higher ranking officer was standing guard. He stepped to one side as Reverend Collins opened the door, still talking to her. 'That sergeant they sent earlier said they'd be taking the body away as soon as they could find the right kind of vehicle. Odd man.

Have you met him? Kind of twitch over one eye, never trust a man who twitches, anyway, here we are, poor chap, we had dinner together last night, the three of us, and then this. Nice young man, studied Greats, we had a rather good chat about Homer…'

He fell silent.

The library was large and surprisingly light, giving out on to the lawn side of the garden rather than the sprawling trees. The young man was lying on his back, next to a chair. One arm was flung outwards, and a book lay just beyond his fingertips. Agatha had the impression that he'd fallen from the chair while reading. His mouth was gaping open as if in horror, or pain. His eyes were staring, pale, blank and absent.

Agatha stood stock still for a few moments. Then she turned to the vicar.

'I think I've seen enough,' she said.

The vicar drew his gaze away from the body. He shook his head. 'Dreadful business,' he said. 'The reputation of the dear old C of E is sticky at the best of times, and this sort of thing really doesn't help at all –'

He was interrupted by the loud ringing of the vicarage doorbell. He frowned as he heard the maid go to open it, took a few steps into the hall, then his face relaxed into a smile. 'Oh, Arthur, of course,' he said, as a tall, smart young man sauntered into the hallway, a shaft of sunlight behind him.

'Terribly sorry, old chap,' the young man was saying. 'Good heavens, what's all this? You look like a funeral party. And you can't move for cars out there…'

'Ah. This is Mr. Sutton. He's working on a painting in the church. We're convinced it's a Holbein but no one will believe us.'

'We'll show 'em,' Arthur Sutton said, with a tap on the vicar's arm. 'So – what's going on?'

Mrs. Ettridge broke the silence. 'A dead body, in the library, that's what's going on.'

'A dead…' He looked from one to the other. 'Is this a joke, Vicar?'

'I'm afraid not. Our young guest seems to have been poisoned at some point last night.'

'Good heavens.' Arthur's jollity seemed to drain from him. 'That nice young man?'

There were nods from the assembled group.

'Poisoned?'

There were more nods.

Arthur frowned. 'They always say it's a woman's weapon, don't they?'

'Well, Mrs. Christie here will know all about that,' the vicar said.

'Are you a poisoner?' Arthur turned to her with an attentive look.

She smiled, shook her head. 'Only in my mind,' she said. His expression was blank, as someone who had no idea who she was, and she felt a sudden relief that here was one person who didn't

12

expect her to be interested in these ghastly events just because of her reputation as a story-teller.

'Oh, but surely you've heard of –' Mrs. Ettridge began to enlighten him, but to Agatha's relief she was interrupted as all eyes turned towards the passageway that led from the kitchen.

A thin young woman had appeared. She came and stood beside Robert, her shoulders hunched, her hands twisting together. She had brown hair that hung in untidy strands around her face, flat shoes, a grey skirt that clung awkwardly around her shins.

Mrs. Ettridge stared at her, then at Robert, waiting for an introduction. At last, Robert said, awkwardly, 'Auntie Sylvia... This is Miss Holgate.'

'Ah, Miss Holgate, there you are.' The vicar's booming voice cut through the silence, and Robert appeared to breathe again. 'This is our little helper, aren't you dear? Terrible time for you to have joined us, of course. But I'm afraid I'm not in control of everything.' He laughed as if he'd made a very good joke.

Miss Holgate looked up at him. 'I've done all those files now, Vicar. I thought I'd leave, if that's all right. What with ...' She inclined her head towards the library door.

'Of course my dear. Very kind of you to come in at all,' the vicar said, 'in the circumstances. Off you go. We'll be back to normal by the morning, you'll see.'

She picked up her hat from the hat-stand, and with a shy backward glance at Robert, she went out of the door, placing her hat on her head as she went.

13

'Bethnal Green,' the vicar said.

'Quite,' Sylvia said. 'I was thinking the same thing myself.'

'Bethnal Green?' Arthur looked from one to the other.

'Mr. Sutton,' the vicar said, 'you'll find there is a network of connections that spreads across the South of England. And at the heart of it, like a benign mother spider, is Mrs. Ettridge here.'

Sylvia gave a smile. 'Well, I do what I can.'

The vicar went on, 'Miss Holgate comes from a family of six, no mother to speak of, it was through Mrs. Ettridge's connections that we found her. And what a helpful young woman she is, too. I've had heaps of papers building up, over decades, they go back years, the previous incumbent did nothing with them …'

'A friend of mine works with the needy folk of London's East End,' Sylvia said. 'I'm glad she found you someone.'

'Miss Holgate has set to with the files. She's a clever young thing under all that shyness.' He turned to Mrs. Ettridge again. 'And you knew this poor dead boy too?' the vicar asked.

'Not really. It just turned out he was doing some of his medical training at one of the clinics there where my friend helps out, that's all.'

'The whole village would fall apart without you, Mrs. Ettridge, the vicar said. 'Even Arthur here depends on you –'

'Only for supplies of turpentine,' Arthur smiled.

'I just happened to have a job lot,' Sylvia said.

Arthur was staring thoughtfully towards the library door. 'Bethnal Green,' he said, again, as the front door swung on its hinges and

Mary appeared. She seemed calmer and more composed, and she smiled at Agatha.

'Everything's all right after all. Phoebe managed to round up both horses. But they're terribly over-excited, we simply must get them back to the stables, and poor Phoebe is very upset about this awful tragedy with the young man, I do think I should get her home. I've told that policeman he can talk to her when her mother's present.'

Agatha moved towards the door. 'I'm heading back too,' she said, firmly.

'But –' Sylvia was giving her a firm look. 'What about Robert?'

Agatha looked at Robert, who returned her gaze.

Mary gave a little wave. 'I must get on with the horses, dear,' she said. 'But I'll see you for our outing, on Wednesday, won't I?'

'Wouldn't miss it for the world.' Agatha returned her wave, then turned back to Robert.

'Dear Mrs. Christie was going to help you talk to the police,' Sylvia interjected.

He turned to her. 'I'm perfectly all right, Auntie Sylvia,' he said. 'And the police have had all the information from me that they require.' He glanced towards the officer, who had returned to his post by the library and who now gave a cheerful nod.

'Oh.' Sylvia stood in the middle of the hall. 'Well, in that case …' Her hands went to her coat pockets, retrieving her gloves once more. The party moved towards the front door. There was a gathering of coats, a picking up of bags, the crunch of shoes on the gravel drive as they left the vicarage. 'Even so, I do think we should visit my friend Mrs. Cohen.'

'Mrs. Cohen?' Agatha said.

'My friend who works so selflessly in the East End clinics. I think she might be able to shed further light on these events. Would tomorrow be convenient for you?'

'Sylvia. You really don't need me,' Agatha said.

Sylvia's eyes were wide with indignation. 'Agatha, dear, you can't leave us now. As far as I can see, the plot is thickening even as we speak.'

Agatha's expression hardened. 'I am not interested in plots,' she said. 'Not real life ones, anyway.'

'You mean, you would be if this was a story, just a work of fiction?' Sylvia's tone had a certain harshness. 'Well, perhaps you should look at it that way,' she said.

'You mean, for you it's just a bit of fun?' Agatha met her gaze.

Sylvia hesitated. 'No, of course not. It's just …'

'I am not a detective,' Agatha Christie said.

'No, of course, I understand that.'

There was a silence. The vicar had gone back indoors. Arthur had disappeared round to his workshop. A chill breeze whispered through the rhododendron bushes.

It was Robert who broke the silence. He had been standing, quietly, behind them, and now he spoke.

'Mrs. Christie,' he said. 'If I might have a word …?'

16

Sylvia flashed him a glance, but he had taken hold of the sleeve of Agatha's coat and now led her away towards the garden.

'I don't know how to begin my explanation,' he said. 'And I don't want to inconvenience you in any way … but there is more to this than it seems. I fear that it is very likely that I shall be inculcated in the death of my friend. I fear that it shall come to pass that the finger of blame will be levelled at my head. And I did not kill him, Mrs. Christie. I am asking you to believe me.'

Agatha took in the intense blue gaze, the thin, nervous face.

'Mr. Sayer,' she began. 'I'm sure there is no question that you killed him.'

His expression was anguished. 'We have been colleagues for these last few months. And very good friends.' He took hold of her hands in both his own. 'Forgive me, Mrs. Christie, but I need your help. You alone can rescue me from this unfortunate situation.'

'Mr. Sayer,' she said. 'I am not a detective.'

'But you are a kind, intelligent woman,' he said. 'And you know an innocent man when you see one.'

'You are rather speaking in riddles,' she said.

'I hope that soon I will be able to speak more clearly,' he replied. 'Please – please come with us to Bethnal Green in the morning.'

In Agatha's mind, she saw the image of her desk, waiting in her sunlit study. She saw the notebooks heaped upon it, the words traced across the paper, and within the words the characters all assembled, all waiting for their story to unfold, all waiting to speak the words

17

that she will place upon their lips. Robert had let go of her hands and stood, waiting too. His eyes were pleading, tearful, almost.

'Tomorrow,' she said to Robert, 'Tomorrow I shall come with you. And then, after that, I shall go back to my work.'

Chapter Three

Sylvia left her at the vicarage gate, pleading errands, 'I'd love to accompany you, Mrs. Christie, but I promised Mrs. Edwards some advice on her delphiniums, and I'm already later than I said I'd be …'

Agatha walked alone along the lane.

This trip to London tomorrow. I could always back out of it, she thought. *I could spend a quiet afternoon in the study, getting to grips with this new novel, and then tomorrow I can really get started on the opening chapters.*

She thought of the young curate, his intense, troubled gaze.

I suppose it won't take long. A morning in London.

It occurred to her that she needed some tea, and Archie was talking about buying a new watch, she could have a look in Burlington Arcade –

A woman ran across her path, pursued by a man. He seemed to be shouting at her, calling her name, 'Bertha – listen to me –'

The woman was tall and dressed in black, her skirts flowing behind her as she ran. The man caught up with her, grabbed her elbow, and she attempted, feebly to shake him off.

Agatha was by now only a few feet away from them.

'May I help?' she said. She realized as she approached that they were both familiar. She'd seen the woman the day before, buying eggs at the dairy. And as for the man, she'd noticed him driving a new and shiny motor-car through the village a couple of times during the previous week.

They both stared at her. The man, with a polite, gentlemanly gaze. The woman, tearful and hostile.

The woman was shaking her head, but the man let go of her elbow and offered his hand to Agatha.

'Clifford Fullerton,' he said. 'And you must be Mrs. Christie.'

She shook the outstretched hand and gave a brief nod.

'And this is Miss Wilkins. I was just offering her a lift home. If you'll excuse us …' His voice tailed away. His hand went back to the woman's arm. 'We really must be going.'

He led Miss Wilkins away towards his motor-car which was parked further up the lane. Her steps were drooping and slow, as she bowed to his will. Agatha watched her get into the passenger seat, watched as he started the engine, revved it loudly, then drove away, up the lane away from the village.

*

The morning dawned drizzly and cold. Agatha saw Archie off to work. She played with little Rosalind, handed her, reluctantly, to Sefton, gave Alice the maid her orders for the day, then gazed with longing at the pile of paper on her desk in the study. There was a letter from her publishers worrying about Belgian characters, what with the memories of the War, and saying that a cheerful British chap might prove more popular. It occurred to her that Inspector Jerome was hardly what one might call cheerful. She was finding his moping around after Bunty Flowers rather wearing. Perhaps once the murder investigation gets under way he'll find some vim, she thought. So far she'd mapped out that it involved two sisters, one of them now grief-stricken. Maybe I should write that scene first, she thought.

She was rather looking forward to sitting down with them again, but she knew that Sylvia would be calling for her to go to the station in half an hour, and she had to find a raincoat, an umbrella and suitable shoes for rain-soaked London streets.

*

The Charterhouse Mother and Baby Clinic was situated within a much older building, tucked away from the busy traffic of the Bethnal Green Road.

'I mean, a medieval gatehouse is all very well, but a clinic really ought to be more hygienic,' Sylvia said, as she strode through the archway, Agatha and Robert close behind. 'I've told Matilda my feelings, and I'm sure she agrees with me. Don't you?' she said, loudly, as a woman approached them, arm outstretched in greeting.

'Don't I what?' Matilda Cohen was tall and upright, her dark hair loosely piled into a bun, her skirt almost at her ankles, with a bright velvet jacket made from fabric that looked as if it had been destined for curtains before being stolen away by a maker of ladies' fashion.

'I was saying …' Sylvia looked around her, as they made their way through the courtyard towards the entrance. 'That you could do with some lovely hygienic new building rather than all this ...'

The courtyard was crowded with families, mothers with prams, some holding their children. Agatha saw faces smudged with grime, wide, hungry eyes.

'We do our best,' was all Matilda would say.

They went through the doorway, which gave on to a wide corridor. This, too, was lined with people, mostly women, the occasional man.

As they walked along the corridor, Mrs. Cohen explained the nature of the clinic's work, the importance of teaching these mothers how to feed their children nutritious food, to teach basic cooking skills so that even on a small income, the family might be able to eat better. Agatha began to feel glad she'd come.

'And dear Cecil was a godsend to us,' Mrs. Cohen was saying. 'I don't know how we'll manage without him. Such terrible news, we were so deeply shocked. Mind you, he was rather distracted these last few days, of course.'

'Distracted?' Agatha asked. They'd reached an office, a small, disorderly space with paper piled on all the furniture, even on the old leather chairs. Another woman was there, with short, grey hair and a neat grey suit. 'This is Mrs. Solomon,' Mrs. Cohen said. 'My cousin.'

Mrs. Solomon laughed, a merry, easy laugh.

Agatha was aware of Robert standing nervously at her side.

'Why was Cecil distracted?' she tried again.

Mrs. Cohen turned to her. 'Oh? I thought you'd know. Breaking off that relationship of his. I think people thought they were engaged, but it was not to be.'

'So terribly sad,' Mrs. Solomon said, serious now. 'He was destined for great things. So talented with the children here, and all the chaps who worked with him at the hospital spoke so highly of him.'

'I was never sure about that woman,' Mrs. Cohen said. 'She was a lot older than he was. If I were his mother, I must say I'd be rather relieved.'

'Oh, me too,' Mrs. Solomon said.

'Not that he had a mother,' Mrs. Cohen said.

A sombre mood settled on the room. 'And of course, we were to blame,' Mrs. Solomon said, suddenly.

'Because they met here,' Mrs. Cohen said.

Mrs. Solomon nodded. 'Miss Wilkins was training as a nurse and did an attachment here. That's how they met.'

'Miss Wilkins?' It was Sylvia who spoke. 'Bertha Wilkins?'

Both women turned to her. They nodded.

Sylvia shifted uncomfortably, and Agatha had the impression that she was not enjoying being told something about the village that she did not already know.

'So, this Cecil,' Sylvia said. 'You looked after him?'

'Well, when someone has so little family of their own –' Mrs. Cohen said.

'– and we have so much to spare,' Mrs. Solomon added. Both women laughed.

'And Miss Holgate?' Agatha asked.

'Miss Holgate?' Mrs. Cohen looked uncomprehending.

'The young lady at the vicarage,' Sylvia prompted. 'They said you'd found her.'

'Oh. Yes. One of our helpers here. You remember,' Mrs. Solomon nudged her cousin. 'Gwendoline. Sweet girl, terribly poor, there was a request from Windlesham Parish for a filing clerk, and we found her the post there.'

'Ah, yes.' Mrs. Cohen glanced at Agatha. 'How awful that this should happen when she's just started. Still, she's made of stern stuff. I'm sure she'll get on with it.'

'If you know of any other likely young women,' Sylvia began, but was interrupted by a knock on the door.

A young man in a white coat put his rather timorous head around the door. 'Ladies,' he began, shyly. 'The doctor is here about the vaccination programme ...'

'Ah yes –'

'Of course –'

There was bustle, busyness, the shifting and sorting of heaps of paper, a move towards the door.

'So kind of you to come,' Mrs. Cohen was saying.

'So kind,' her cousin echoed.

'Such a waste of a talented young man,' Mrs. Cohen said, shaking hands, moving away along the corridor.

Agatha, Robert and Sylvia found themselves outside, standing by the medieval gate.

'Well.' Sylvia pulled on her gloves, emphatically. She began to walk ahead, leading the way towards the main road.

Robert turned to Agatha. 'I knew it,' he said. 'I knew that something had happened with Bertha.' His voice was deliberately low so that only she could hear. He stood close beside her and continued, 'I believe Bertha to be unstable. Twice now she's come to the vicarage, very upset, wanting to speak to the vicar. They closet themselves away, and she leaves about half an hour later, creeping out of the kitchen garden like a ghost. Frankly,' he said, turning to follow Sylvia, 'I was glad when Cecil said he wasn't going to have anything more to do with her. But then … but then things got so much more serious. So dreadfully serious …' His voice cracked. Agatha got the impression his eyes had filled with tears, but he was ahead of her now, catching up with Sylvia, and she couldn't be sure.

'We really are none the wiser.' Sylvia's voice carried above the noise of the London traffic, the horses, carts, and motor-cars. 'Apart from this matter of a romantic liaison, which I have to say I knew nothing about … I can't imagine it was that important,' she finished. 'Miss Wilkins has only recently come to stay in her poor sister's house. I can't see how she believed herself to be engaged to Mr. Coates after such a short time.'

'They met here, though,' Agatha said. 'Isn't that what Mrs. Cohen said? It might have been going on longer.'

Sylvia considered this, standing stock still amidst the city crowds. Then she shrugged, as if the very idea was now dismissed. 'I think we should hail a cab, don't you? We're on the wrong side of town here, and it would be nice to get back to civilization.'

*

25

That evening the rain eased and the sky cleared. Archie lit a fire in the sitting room grate. They sat in silence, enjoying the after-dinner quiet. Rosalind was long since tucked up and sleeping in the nursery and Peter the dog was dozing on the hearthrug.

Agatha put down her notebook and stared at the low, flickering flames. Robert had been silent all the way home, as the suburbs of London had given way to the open green Berkshire fields, and she'd wondered why he had been so keen to visit the clinic, and why he'd been so insistent that she come too.

'I suppose you can get some ideas from all this.' Her husband's voice interrupted her thoughts.

She looked up. 'From all what?'

'This adventure with the poor boy at the vicarage. If your publishers want another of your books, Thingie and Whatsername, or that French chap –'

'He's Belgian,' she said, firmly.

'Well, there you are,' he said. 'A body in the library. A secret love affair. A poor young man's life cut short …'

Her voice was firm. 'Archie, I make it up. I've had no need to borrow from real life. And I don't intend to start now.'

He blinked at her tone. After a moment, he went back to reading the paper. She listened to the rustle as he folded the pages back. She looked down at her notebook. The page was almost blank, but she'd written the words, 'creeping like a ghost'.

Chapter Four

The clear night gave way to a cloudless morning. Agatha walked towards the railway station. Her mother had admired a lavender plant in her garden on a recent visit, and Agatha had promised her that she'd try to find one for her garden too, and she was on her way to ask Mr. Selby about a cutting.

The path led out of the village and up the hill. There was spring sunshine and birdsong. 'Now, you will make sure you don't tie yourself to your desk, won't you?' Archie's parting words rang in her mind. He'd been saying such things rather frequently, as if the idea of his wife sitting at her writing desk was somehow troubling to him. But he'd greeted her recent modest success with pleasure, and his calculations of her potential royalties bordered on obsessive.

I will tell him I walked all the way to the garden nurseries and back, she thought.

Ahead of her a figure crossed her path. Agatha recognised the long black skirts, the bowed head. This time Miss Wilkins had a black bonnet shading her face against the sunlight. She stayed ahead of her, walking fast, and Agatha quickened her pace to keep her in sight.

The path led out of the village, towards the higher ground where the dairy cattle grazed. Miss Wilkins was walking with purpose, and now they were at the walls of Hainault Hall. Agatha expected her to go through the gate, but Miss Wilkins passed the gate and continued on the path, which was by now no more than a rough bridle track.

The trees were more sparse, and the path came out onto a field, a patch of overgrown green. Bertha Wilkins stopped. She stood still, standing in the sunlight at the end of the field. The spring flowers were out. Watching her, the thin dark figure against the blue sky, the daffodils bright against the green of the grass, Agatha felt herself come to her senses, felt herself intruding on this poor woman's distress. Fearful of being seen, she turned away, and began to descend the path back to the village.

Someone was standing at the gate of Hainault Hall.

'I say. Mrs. Christie,' a male voice said.

Agatha recognized the artist from the vicarage the day before.

'Mr. Sutton,' Agatha said. 'Good morning.'

'What brings you up here?' His smile was warm, as he raised his hat to her. It was a tweed cap which matched his jacket. His trousers were dark with odd splashes of colour, which she realized as she drew nearer, were paint.

She was aware of her own confusion, wondering what to say, but before she could speak he said, 'Did Bertha bring you here? It wouldn't surprise me. She's obsessed with that gravestone, poor woman.'

'Gravestone?'

'The old church yard, up the hill. It was the family chapel in the old days. Perhaps you remember?'

Agatha shook her head. 'Before my time, I fear,' she said.

'You haven't been in the village long, then?'

'Only eighteen months. We were in London before.'

There was a silence. He had replaced his cap on his head, and now he scanned the distant horizon, before turning to her once more. 'She's moved into her sister's house, down the hill there. Her sister recently died. And they say she was in love with that poor Mr. Coates too. A double blow for her, to lose him. Sometimes life deals people a very harsh hand, wouldn't you say?'

He turned and began to walk along the drive, and Agatha fell into step beside him.

'I'm sorry I didn't know who you were,' he said, in his easy, friendly manner. 'Yesterday. They told me afterwards that you're a writer.'

'Yes,' she said.

'It must be very enjoyable,' he said.

She wondered what to say, but he was still speaking. 'I feel I've landed on my feet here,' he was saying. 'I've lived in villages before, where people will cross the street rather than talk to an incomer, but Sunningdale seems completely different.' They'd reached the end of the drive, and the house stood before them.

Hainault Hall had been empty for some years, and even now, as Agatha surveyed it, it had a neglected look. The fine yellow stone was shadowed with patches of moss. There were visible gaps between the tiles on the roof.

'I know, I know,' he said. 'I've got my work cut out, haven't I? But I intend to restore it to its former glory. But that's what I mean, about this village. No one seems to resent my having taken on the house. I've had offers of help from all manner of people. Mr. Selby said he'd cut back the hedges for me when he gets a moment. And your friend –'

'Mrs. Ettridge,' Agatha said.

'Yes. She said if I need any wood there's a church in the next village getting rid of its pews. And then it turns out she knows Phoebe Banks whom I met a couple of weeks ago – she's working as a help for Mrs. Garvey, in between being at the stables, of course horses are her first love but Mrs. Garvey's boy has got whooping cough at the moment, everyone's been very worried about him.' Arthur continued to chat as they walked around the front of the house. 'To be honest, Mrs. Christie –' He turned to her, his expression open, his blonde hair pale in the sunlight – 'I'm rather keen on Phoebe. Very keen, in fact. We went up to London, to the theatre, last week, and I can't have had such an enjoyable evening for years. But I don't imagine she's interested in a penniless artist.'

'Hardly penniless,' Agatha heard herself say, as her gaze alighted once more on the beauty of the building behind him.

He shook his head. 'I was lucky. An unwanted, neglected house. The lady owner had had nothing to do with it, inherited it from her aunt. She was clearly relieved, and I think, rather amazed, that I wanted it.' He waved a hand towards it. 'I have very little money, but every last penny of mine will go towards restoring this house to its former glory. I'm taking a chance, I have to say. Which is another reason Phoebe won't look twice at me, theatre or not. I can gamble on my future worth, but I can't expect her to … Well, back to work. For both of us, I shouldn't wonder.'

'Yes,' she said, with a certain reluctance.

He walked with her back towards the gate. 'Perhaps yours is easier than mine,' he said, suddenly. 'Work, I mean. It doesn't depend on anything other than itself. Whereas mine …' Again, the warm expression, a touch of pink in his cheeks, a sudden awkwardness. 'I have this terrible sense that I have to get it right. Restoration. I can't risk betraying the original, and I find it almost paralyzing. What if it's too new, too crisp? What if the materials I'm using now are somehow inappropriate, compared to what the artist used?' They were out on the lane now, and Agatha was aware of the scent of wildflowers in the hedgerows. Arthur was still speaking. 'You see, you can start with a clean slate. Whereas I am always worried by the feeling that I might be making something new rather than being true to what an artist so much greater than myself created all those years ago …' He broke off, his attention caught by something further up the hill.

Bertha Wilkins was walking slowly towards them. As she approached, she raised her eyes to them both, and murmured, 'Good morning, Mr. Sutton. Good morning Mrs. Christie,' as she passed.

They watched her as she reached the bottom of the path, her small, quick steps in her lace-up boots, the weight of her skirt against her ankles.

31

Arthur turned back to Agatha. 'Or, then again, perhaps I'm wrong,' he said to her. 'Perhaps your work is also about restoring something that already exists. Telling a story whose truth resides in real life.'

She smiled at him. 'Having a natural curiosity about people is one thing. But what I write is fiction. Of that I am entirely clear.'

'Well ...' He held out his hand. 'No doubt we'll see each other again soon. This awful business at the vicarage ...'

She shook his hand briefly. 'Awful,' she agreed.

'I'm working there later today. You're very welcome to pop in. I could show you the Holbein. The vicar's hoping the money from it will pay for the restoration of the church bell, you know. You're very welcome to have a look.'

'Thank you,' she said. 'I'd like that.'

Agatha turned and began to walk away, down the hill. In her mind she still saw her, the slim black silhouette against the sky, the green grass and the yellow flowers.

Art and life, she thought. *Yesterday I wrote about a woman who had lost her much-loved sister. And today I hear about this Miss Wilkins, and her grief at her sister's death. Fiction, and reality. And where does the truth lie?*

*

Mr. Selby was only too pleased to talk about lavender cuttings, the difference between French and English plants, 'I'd go for the English myself, you know where you are with it, people like the fuller flowers of the French one but it always seems to me it's putting on airs and graces ...'

32

Agatha walked back to the village, having agreed that he would deliver her a cutting in time for her mother's next visit.

As she reached the main street, there was the loud revving of a motor car and the crunch of brakes. 'Mrs. Christie,' a voice said. She felt she was getting rather tired of these interruptions to her thoughts, and turned to find Mr. Fullerton in his shiny motor-car, having pulled up beside her.

'I was hoping to bump into you,' he said, his voice raised against the loud revving of the engine. 'You're just the person who can help.'

'Help?' she asked, weakly, aware that Alice and Sefton would be expecting her back for lunch with Rosalind, and also aware that she was very hungry.

'Poor Bertha is beside herself. She's waiting for the knock at the door at any time.'

Agatha's thoughts had been circling her new novel. She had been thinking about the bereaved sister, imagining a scene where she stands near a graveyard. 'I really can't imagine that that has anything to do with me,' she said.

'Oh, but it does. Your friend Mary Ansell employs young Phoebe Banks doesn't she, at the stables?'

'Well, yes, I believe so …'

'Well, Bertha says that Phoebe will have seen something, something that will clear her name. Only Phoebe won't say anything, because of course, the poor dead chap was in love with Phoebe, wasn't he, having broken off his relationship with Bertha in order to be with Phoebe. So there is a terrible stand-off between the two women. Bertha is furious with Phoebe, just as she was with Cecil when he told her he couldn't continue their relationship. And Phoebe is young and pretty, and Bertha is not in the first flush of youth, but she has great virtues, great virtues …' He stopped, smoothed his hand across the steering wheel. 'Between you and me, Mrs. Christie, it is my good fortune that poor Cecil didn't see what a wonderful woman Bertha Wilkins is.'

'I still don't see what this has got to do with me.' Agatha took a step away from the kerb.

His arm reached out and grabbed her hand. His expression was intense and his eyes were dark as they searched her face. 'I fear that a grave injustice will take place,' he said. 'And you are singularly well-placed to prevent it. Come with me, please, to the stables, and we can both talk to Phoebe.'

Agatha sighed. She was aware of her increasing hunger. She was aware too, that life at home would continue whether she was there or not. Rosalind would be fed, Sefton would put her down for her nap, the dogs would be walked by Alice, who adored them …

She got into Clifford's car and they set off for the stables.

Chapter Five

There was something comforting about stables, Agatha thought, as they closed the rickety gate behind them and walked into the yard. The warm, farmyard smell. The quiet activity of the grooms. The way the horses whinnied and gossiped gently from their stalls. Clifford strode ahead of her, just as Phoebe emerged from the tack room.

There was no doubting that Phoebe was a very pretty girl. She greeted Clifford with a toss of blonde hair and a flirtatious smile. She was small and trim, and even in jodhpurs and an old sweater she looked somehow well-dressed.

'Miss Banks,' he said. 'I want you to meet Mrs. Christie. She's helping us with this awful business at the vicarage.'

Agatha felt rather than saw the urgent glance he flashed at Phoebe. In response Phoebe fixed her with a sweet, blue gaze. 'I know Mrs. Christie,' she said.

'We're both friends of Mrs. Ansell,' Agatha said.

'Ah.' Clifford looked between them. 'Everyone knows everyone in this village.' He turned back to Phoebe. 'How's the whooping cough?'

'Oh, it's been terrible,' Phoebe said with a heavy sigh. 'Poor Jack has been so poorly. But the doctor said at least no one else seems to have got it. And Mrs. Garvey said they were just lucky that Cecil was so helpful with it all, bringing medicine from London and all that. She says he saved her Jack's life, and she's terribly cut up about him having been … murdered … in that way …' Her voice faltered. She turned her wide blue eyes to Clifford.

'Mrs. Christie has met Bertha,' he said, and the words felt weighted with meaning.

'Oh.' Phoebe glanced at Agatha.

'Shall we walk up to the field?' Clifford took her arm, and the three of them drifted away from the yard, along the path towards the grazing field. It was warm and sunny, and they watched the horses as they contentedly nibbled at the grass.

'She was so cross with Cecil,' Phoebe blurted out, once they were away from the yard. 'Bertha was. She was telling him he didn't deserve to live. She said she'd kill him herself given the chance.'

'When was this?' Agatha turned towards her.

Phoebe was leaning on the gate. 'Monday,' she said, and seemed to shudder at the memory.

'And what had brought about this terrible rage?' Agatha asked.

Phoebe glanced briefly at Clifford, before replying, 'Well, because she felt jilted, I suppose.'

'I see. And how long had they been, shall we say, seeing each other?'

'I don't rightly know. All I know is Cecil wasn't that interested in her, you can always tell when a young man *is* interested, can't you?'

'Can you?' Agatha asked.

'Oh yes. Well, at least, I can.' This was said with a certain pride.

Clifford smiled.

'And who was Cecil interested in?' Agatha asked.

Phoebe looked down at her muddy boots. She blushed. 'Me,' she said.

'But lots of people are interested in you,' Clifford said. His tone was avuncular, and Agatha realized that his attitude to Phoebe was not that of an interested suitor but more a kindly, older relative. 'The young man of Hainault Hall, for example …'

She blushed some more. 'Arthur,' she said. 'We had such a lovely evening. He took me to the theatre …'

'However,' Clifford was suddenly serious, 'Bertha threatened Cecil. And when she realized he was keen on you, she began to threaten you too, didn't she?'

Phoebe's sweet blushing faded. She nodded.

'All sorts of threats,' Clifford said.

'She didn't mean them …'

'I think she did.' Clifford turned to Agatha. 'This is my fear, Mrs. Christie. That Bertha is not acting in a rational way. That she's a danger to others. And certainly, most importantly, she's a danger to herself.'

'Cecil had a secret.' Phoebe's voice cut through the gentle rural sounds around them. 'That's why she was angry with him. Not just about me, but because there was something he wouldn't tell her. On Sunday, he'd said to Gwendoline, Miss Holgate, that he wanted to talk to her alone. She told me. We've become friends, recently, she loves the horses, she never learned to ride but I've promised to teach her. Anyway, she mentioned it on Sunday evening, we were laughing about it, we had no idea it would cause …' Her face darkened. 'We didn't think it was so serious.'

'And Cecil?' Agatha watched her, her clear, innocent face, her puzzlement that something so awful should happen.

'He'd come to stay with Robert at the vicarage, his friend from London, that's how we met in the first place, when he paid a visit here, and he'd promised to come back and now he had. I was so pleased when I heard I'd be seeing him again …' She sniffed, then went on, 'He said he'd come to Mrs. Garvey's when I'd finished for the day and we could go for a walk, this was on Monday. So he met me, and we started down the lane, and then Miss Wilkins appears from nowhere and she's shouting, so angry, I was quite scared, wasn't I?' She turned to Clifford as if for verification.

'And this was when she uttered all these threats?' Agatha prompted.

Phoebe nodded. 'She told him she'd kill him.'

'And the secret?'

Phoebe glanced at Clifford again. He seemed to give a nod, as if in permission. 'That's what she said,' Phoebe went on. 'She said, "What have you told Miss Holgate that you can't tell me?" And he said it didn't concern her, and she got even more angry, and then eventually she stomped away down the hill, but she was still talking to herself …' She sniffed again. 'It's just so awful that he's gone.' She lifted tearful eyes to Clifford. 'Dear Cecil. I didn't know him

38

that well but he was the nicest, kindest young man you could hope to meet, and the idea that he'd be poisoned in that terrible way …'

Clifford patted her arm. 'Let's go back to the yard,' he said. 'You can take comfort in the horses.'

She nodded, brushed tears from her eyes. 'I'm due at Mrs. Garvey's soon,' she said.

'I'll drive you up there.' Clifford gently took Phoebe's arm.

They walked back to the yard. Agatha said her goodbyes, and a few minutes later was ringing the doorbell of the vicarage.

Chapter Six

The door was opened by Gwendoline Holgate herself. She was still in grey, but today she looked tidier, and more composed, and she stood quietly aside to let Agatha in.

'Is Mr. Sutton here?' Agatha asked her.

Gwendoline shook her head. 'He's due later on, Ma'am, but he's not here yet.'

'Ah.' Agatha studied her surroundings. The vicarage hall still seemed dark and gloomy, not helped by the overgrown trees that loomed outside.

Agatha looked at Miss Holgate. 'I wonder if I might ask you,' she said, 'about Cecil Coates?'

The young woman fixed her with a deep brown gaze. 'You're the one who writes stories, aren't you?'

Agatha gave a reluctant nod.

'And you know Robert's godmother, Mrs. Ettridge?'

Another reluctant nod.

'It's because of her friends in Bethnal Green that I got this job,' Gwendoline said. 'That's what Robert said. When the vicar said he needed someone, that's who he went to and they found me the place here.'

'And are you glad they did?' Agatha asked.

The stern features broke into a smile. 'Oh, yes, Ma'am. Very glad. I was working in the school there, and it was very hard.'

'Shall we go and sit somewhere?'

The smile faded. 'Well … if you don't mind, Ma'am, it'll have to be the kitchen. I haven't set foot in the library since … well … and the vicar tends to rest at this time so we can't disturb him.'

Agatha followed her down the little passageway into the kitchen. It was lighter here, and warm, with a residual smell of something like fresh bread.

Miss Holgate flopped on to a chair, as if the air had been let out of her. 'I try to be brave, I really do. But it's been so difficult. And all this has made it a hundred times worse. When I was at school, I thought, nothing can be as bad as this. When I leave school, I will understand about life, and there'll be music, and dancing, and I can go to the theatre, and wear lovely clothes, and I'll drink tea from proper cups, and when people bring cakes they'll be on a pink cake stand. And now …' She raised a tearful face to Agatha. 'And it's even worse for Robert.' Her voice wobbled at his name. 'And the awful thing is, it's all my fault.'

'Your fault?' Agatha sat down gently beside her.

She nodded, her eyes welling with tears.

'Miss Banks told me …' Agatha began. 'Miss Banks told me that Cecil had wanted to talk to you.'

'Oh, if only he'd got the chance. If only I knew what it was.' It was a heartfelt cry. 'He meant no harm. I just wish Robert had trusted him. I met him just after Christmas, just after my appointment here,

41

he'd come to see Robert. We got on very well, me and Cecil, we'd have a laugh, you know. A smile lightened her features briefly, then faded. 'I didn't like him in the way Robert thought. I really didn't. Robert has always been the only man for me. I just assumed he knew that. So I didn't notice how jealous Robert was becoming. And then on Monday night, Robert challenged me. He said, "Cecil came here to see you, not me, didn't he?" And I didn't know what to say, because … because it was true, you see.'

'So you don't know what Cecil wanted to tell you?'

She shook her head. 'I'll never know. He'd arrived at the weekend, and on the Sunday he took me on one side and said he had something very important to talk to me about. But Robert made sure we were never alone together, and then … and then …' She began to sob, pulling out an embroidered handkerchief, dabbing at her eyes. 'He was like a friend to me. And now he's gone. And I know it's something to do with me.'

She was still sobbing when the green baize door was quietly pushed open. Arthur was standing there. 'Forgive me,' he began. 'I came to do some work on the painting.'

'Miss Holgate has been very kind.' Agatha got to her feet. 'But I ought to be going.'

The young woman dried her tears. 'I've got work to do too. The vicar wanted his sermon typed up and I've only just begun.'

'Come and see the painting.' Arthur smiled at Agatha.

After assurances from Gwendoline that she was all right, really, Agatha followed Arthur out into the kitchen corridor. He led the way out to the garden door, through the vegetable patch, and out to an outbuilding.

'Rather of a compromise, keeping the painting here, but the vicar assures me he'll hang it properly as soon as I've finished.' He pushed the door open.

Agatha's eyes adjusted to the gloom.

'They say there were soldiers housed here on manoeuvres,' Arthur said. 'Not sure I believe it myself.'

Agatha saw a high-ceilinged, barn-like space with a smooth wood floor and windows all around the upper edge. Large hulks of farm machinery lurked in the shadows, some covered by rough tarpaulins. A shaft of sunlight cut through the gloom, a beam of light across the old wood floor, illuminating a large gold frame at the end of the space.

They approached the painting.

'You won't see much,' Arthur said. 'It's been very badly damaged, and the paint is very dark. It's a portrait of a man, probably from about 1530, maybe a bit later.'

Agatha looked. The whole painting appeared as a cracked, faded veneer. But the edge of the man's face was illumined, and the collar of his coat had a few patches of a bright, rust-red colour. His eyes shone expressively, although as Agatha peered closer she could see it was a clever arrangement of white pigment in the midst of dark brown.

'It must be him,' Arthur was saying. 'So gifted. The attention to detail … The vicar thinks so too. The vicar's hoping it will show one of the saints, but I'm sure this is a secular creation.'

'An act of faith,' Agatha said. 'Of believing in one's art.' She stared at the painting.

'Not necessarily. They did as they were told. Just as we do,' he said.

A rustling above them interrupted their conversation. 'Bats,' Arthur said. 'I'm keeping them off this end of the building. You can see why I want to get this into the church sharpish.'

He bent to the painting. He picked up a tool, a tiny scalpel, and began to scrape away at one edge of it. 'Personally I'd rather this was a society portrait,' he said. 'Any faith I had, I rather lost it in these last few years.'

'Were you …?' Agatha hesitated.

'The fields of Flanders,' he said. 'Not a place to sustain any belief in a God who loves us. What about you?'

'My husband …' she began. 'He fought, yes.'

'You're lucky he survived.' Arthur put down the scalpel and chose another.

'Yes,' she said. 'I suppose I am.'

'I have felt burdened, at times,' he said. 'The souls of the departed…' The instrument scraped rhythmically against the aged layers.

'I'm going to a séance,' Agatha said. 'Tomorrow.'

'That Russian woman? I heard them talking about her at the Hare and Hounds.'

'My friend Mary insisted …' She saw the red of the coat begin to emerge. She wondered why she'd felt moved to confide in Arthur about her spiritualism.

'False comfort,' he said. 'It's bad enough, grief, without being told lies about the hereafter.'

Agatha turned to him. 'I don't think Mme. Litvinoff thinks it's lies,' she said.

'Even if she means well –' He put down the scalpel. 'It's wrong to give people false hope.'

Agatha took a step back. 'It will be very beautiful,' she said. 'When you've finished your work.'

He smiled. 'I hope so.'

'I really have to go,' she said. Agatha found she was feeling faint, whether from the stale air in the barn or the lack of lunch, she wasn't sure.

'Do let me show you out,' he said.

They walked back into the house, and out into the hall.

'I wouldn't worry too much about Miss Holgate,' Arthur said. 'I think she feels all this more keenly than she needs. And anyway, she has Robert to look after her. He's a good man.'

Agatha nodded.

'And do come back and see the painting. Whenever you like.'

There were thanks and goodbyes and then she was outside.

It had clouded over and the air was humid. Agatha walked away from the vicarage with a sense of heaviness.

Ahead of her, there was shouting. A woman's voice. She rounded the corner to see Bertha Wilkins, striding along the main street, shouting, apparently to no one in particular.

'He'll have asked her to marry him,' she was saying. Her voice was loud and hoarse. 'Cecil will have asked Phoebe to marry him. Fat lot of good it'll do her now …' Her words were followed by a cackle of laughter.

'Miss Wilkins …' Agatha approached her.

Bertha glared up at her from under the black rim of her bonnet. A stray lock of hair blew across her face in the sticky breeze, and she brushed it away.

'What do you want?' She stared angrily at Agatha. 'You come to ask me nosy questions too?'

'No, not at all.'

'Well, then, you can leave me alone, can't you.'

A cyclist came down the hill fast, and narrowly missed her, shouting warnings as he passed.

'Miss Wilkins, please –' Agatha took hold of her arm.

She snatched her hand away. 'Don't you touch me.' She laughed, a harsh, mirthless laugh. 'You don't know where I've been.' She turned, suddenly, and ran off, leaving the path, taking the path across the rain-soaked fields.

Agatha watched her go.

It was time to stop, she thought. It was time to retreat from these events at the vicarage.

She wondered what her husband would make of all this. He too would advise her to keep a distance. 'Village politics,' he'd always say, with a tone of disdain. 'We're not born to all that.' Perhaps he'd say the same of murder, hiding behind his newspaper as he always seemed to do these days.

He's right, of course. I will go back home. I will have something to eat. And then I will go back to my desk and stay there.

In her mind was the image of a woman in black, standing by a gravestone. The strange woman who lives alone at the edge of the village, troubled by the souls of the departed. *I shall call her Dorothea.*

Agatha hurried towards her home. She had a sense of the story emerging, tugging at her, waiting for her to put pen to paper.

Chapter Seven

Inspector Jerome followed Dorothea along the pathway by the cemetery. It was raining, and he was not in a good mood. He'd encountered the elder Miss Flowers only ten minutes before, and he so wanted to ask after her younger sister, Bunty

A ringing at the doorbell made Agatha put down her pen with a sigh. The rain she'd been writing was echoed by the real morning rain which now hammered against the windows. She wondered about pretending to be out, but the dogs were barking, and Alice was nowhere to be seen, and so she dragged herself to the front door.

It was Sylvia. She seemed to be struggling to speak.

'I'm working,' Agatha said, before she could say anything.

Mrs. Ettridge looked terrible, ashen-faced, her hair awry, bare headed, not even wearing gloves.

'What is it?' Agatha was aware of a rising sense of anxiety.

'She's dead.' Sylvia's voice was barely audible.

'Dead? Who's dead?'

'Phoebe.' The name was almost lost in a sob.

Agatha stood to one side, gestured to her neighbour to follow her. She pulled up a chair in the hall, and sat down next to her.

'They found her this morning,' Sylvia said. 'Her mother's beside herself. Been looking all night, she didn't come home, most out of character, they've been searching the village. They found her in the little summerhouse behind the graveyard, just lying there. Same thing.' Her voice was shaking.

'Same thing?'

'Poisoned.'

The shock of this word was followed by silence.

'Who found her?' Agatha asked, after a moment.

Sylvia composed herself, settled her voice. 'Well, that's the very peculiar thing. Miss Holgate found her. She led the police to her. She was the last person to see her alive, it seems. And when the police questioned her, she said, they'd been together, last night, in the old summerhouse. Of course she's very, very upset. Robert is trying to console her, but there's a limit to what the poor man can do. Between you and me, I'm wondering whether to advise him to keep a bit of a distance.' She rummaged in her pockets and produced a pair of gloves, which she proceeded to snap firmly on to her elegant fingers. 'And Miss Wilkins is nowhere to be found either,' Sylvia added, her voice now firm.

Agatha could hear the echo, in her mind, of a raucous laugh. A woman in black, fleeing across muddy fields.

'The village is swarming with police,' Sylvia was saying. The colour had returned to her cheeks. 'I told them that nothing would be too much trouble, and all they have to do is ask. I offered your services too,' she added, getting to her feet.

Reluctantly, Agatha took her coat from the stand in the hall. The humid, cloudy weather had persisted, and once again she felt burdened with a sense of dread.

The swarm of police turned out to be two. The sergeant looked familiar, from his place outside the vicarage. But with him stood a large, dapper man, with a bowler hat and a cane. 'Inspector Mallatratt,' he boomed, approaching with outstretched hand. 'You must be Mrs. Christie.'

'She is,' Sylvia interjected.

'I read your latest,' he was saying. 'I have a few points to make, although of course, now is not the time. But procedurally, there are just a few things I'd put right if I were you. For a start, the way we work as a team … Ah, Sergeant,' he said, as a third man approached him. 'Any sign at Miss Wilkins' residence?'

'Not a thing, Sir. Bed not been slept in.'

Agatha thought about the evening before, the dusk settling across the fields, Bertha's white-faced rage.

Sylvia adjusted her hat on her head. 'Well,' she said. 'Poor Bertha. I mean, we all of us want to kill people at times. But to actually do it…' She gave a brisk sigh.

The Inspector threw her a sharp look. 'Innocent until proven guilty, Madam,' he said. 'That's the British way.'

'Of course, Inspector.'

'As Mrs. Christie here knows all too well. You get that part of it right, I'll give you that.' He nodded towards Agatha.

It appeared to be praise. She gave him a brief smile of acknowledgement.

'We must get on,' Inspector Mallatratt said. 'If you hear anything, you'll tip us the wink, won't you?'

'Oh yes,' Sylvia said with enthusiasm.

'I may be a Londoner, but I know what these English villages are like. Everyone knows everyone, eh?'

'Oh, yes,' Sylvia said, again.

With a formal click of his heels he was gone, following his sergeant up the hill towards the Miss Wilkins' house.

'Well.' Sylvia's gaze followed him. 'We'll just have to wait for news.' She eyed her friend. 'You'd have thought he'd have managed to be more polite about your writing. Manners go a long way, that's what I was always told.' She tucked a stray lock of hair under her hat. 'Oh well. Better get back. I was half-way through a batch of pastry.' She strode away up the high street.

The sky had cleared, with patches of blue promising an end to the rain, a sense of spring in the air again.

Agatha found herself thinking of her story, of Inspector Jerome and his rather clumsy questioning of poor Dorothea Child. She felt uneasy, as if her work was somehow out of place now, in the midst of these events.

A real death. Two, now. And both poisoned.

She took the lane away from the village towards home.

There was a shout from behind her.

'Mrs. Christie.' She turned to see Arthur approaching. At least, it looked like Arthur. His face was streaming with tears.

'You've heard?' His voice was rough with weeping. 'Phoebe.' The name was choked in his throat. 'I can't believe it. I can't believe anything like that could have happened to her. The two of them, Miss Holgate and dear Phoebe happily at supper, and then she dies like that … How could it have happened? How?' His eyes were dark with tears. 'Last week, she and I …' He turned to her again. 'I thought she was my future,' he said. 'I know it sounds hopelessly romantic, but I thought …' His words tailed away.

She placed a maternal hand on his arm. 'It's terrible news,' she said.

He looked at her, through tears. 'Village life,' he said, with sudden viciousness. 'I should never have left the city. This hope of a new start, that house I would have called my home, damned before I even had a chance …' He dashed at his tears with his hand. 'I'm sorry …'

'No need to be sorry,' she said, gently.

'Men aren't supposed to weep,' he said.

'Oh, I think the rules have changed,' she said. 'I think the War changed all that.'

He looked up at her. 'A chance of happiness,' he said. 'After so much suffering …' A new harshness crossed his face. 'I will not be denied,' he said. 'My home. My art …' He touched her arm, briefly. 'You're right, Mrs. Christie,' he said. 'We cannot give up, when so many have died for us.' He raised his arm in a half salute, then walked away.

Agatha made her way towards her home. The sun was warm upon her face, and the crocuses made splashes of purple and yellow in the fields, but the prospect of Inspector Jerome getting anywhere, with either his investigation, or in his romance with Bunty Flowers, seemed even further away.

The vicarage appeared to have a different police officer, standing guard at the gate. He tipped his hat to her. She thought about the vicar, tucked away inside. Poor Miss Holgate, trying to do her job, rescued from her life of poverty, and now surrounded by tragedy. Her sense of guilt, too. 'It's all my fault,' she'd said.

And Robert, hovering, concerned, sharing a worry that he too was somehow implicated in Cecil's death.

And now Phoebe.

An image appeared of her lithe, blonde prettiness, her sweet blue gaze.

Real murder, Agatha thought. *Real life. No order, no resolution, just a grieving mother living in an English village.*

In her mind was the Holbein. Arthur's delicate working, as the sunlight glinted on the golden frame; the truth so painstakingly uncovered.

At home there was only absence. Her husband, so distant, so preoccupied. Her writing, the heap of paper on her desk, all those words just to tell an empty make-believe.

She turned from her home and headed away, up the hill, feeling the warmth of the sunlight on her face. She was aware of footsteps behind her. Heavy, male footsteps. She turned.

'Oh. Mr. Fullerton,' she said.

With a murmured greeting, Clifford Fullerton fell into step beside her. It occurred to her that he must have followed her, that he must have been lurking by the vicarage and seen her pass.

For a while they walked in silence. Agatha, who had had no purpose in her walk, wondered where Clifford thought they were going.

'The graves,' he said, as if in answer. 'The dead.' His voice was grim. His face looked drawn and shadowed. 'This Russian woman,' he began. 'Raising false hopes.'

'Mme. Litvinoff?' Agatha wondered what he meant.

He nodded, forcefully. 'There are posters everywhere. But the dead can tell us nothing. We are stranded here, the other side, willing them to speak. But they are silent. No amount of Cossack glamour can make things otherwise.'

'That's what Mr. Sutton said,' she said.

'Arthur?' He turned to her, sharply.

'About false hope,' she added. 'And séances. I told him I was going –'

'You?' It was almost a shout.

She blinked.

'I'd have expected better of you,' he said.

They walked on in silence. The lane led past the grounds of Hainault House, through an avenue of trees, and then out to the open fields. Clifford stopped, then turned onto a track to the right. He walked with purpose, and she followed him.

'She didn't do it.' He stopped on the narrow path and faced her. 'Bertha. She is incapable of it.'

'They're looking for her –' Agatha began.

'She makes it so difficult for herself,' he said. 'But however angry, however abandoned, however vengeful ...' He shook his head. 'Poisoning, you see. It takes planning. It takes organization. She is incapable of such things ...' He turned away and began to walk again. Agatha followed just behind, as the track was so narrow.

'She is an impoverished woman,' he said. 'She grew up with so little. That's the problem with this country. Working men and women crushed into cauldrons of bad air and poverty, you find it in the North Country, in London's East End, in our dockyards and factory towns. Just so that you people can live your clean, well-mannered lives ...'

He had changed, she realized. The neat vowel sounds had roughened, the smart jacket looked somehow borrowed.

'Why are you so angry?' she asked him.

He stopped and turned to her. His gaze was fierce and honest. 'You may call it anger,' he began. 'I call it simply seeing things as they are. Our fellow countrymen are suffering, dying on battlefields, crushed to death in mills, and yet there they are still, the land-owning class, dancing at the Savoy, drinking champagne, still living as if the blood of heroes isn't lapping at their feet ...' He seemed about to say more, but they were at a gate and he stopped, then pushed it open. 'The dead,' he said. 'They may be silent, but their stories still speak to us.'

55

She realized they were at the top of the hill, and below them lay the graveyard where she had seen Bertha, yesterday morning.

'Look –' He waved towards the long grass and wildflowers. 'This was once the churchyard, until the vicar acquired that more level field the other side of the church. So now, these just rest here, untended. The unkempt graves of those too poor to pay for upkeep. Bertha's sister is buried up here somewhere. And here, look …' He took a few steps away from the path. 'This – this is my mother's grave.' Agatha saw a plain, grey stone, a name, some dates. 'She worked in the old house, Hainault House, when it was owned by the Taptons. She knew Sir Wyndham well, and his first wife. And look – that first wife, she's buried here too. Dympna, Lady Tapton.'

The stone was pale gold, and elegantly inscribed.

'She died in childbirth,' Clifford said. 'And then her twins died a few weeks later. A tragedy. Poor Sir Wyndham married again, a year or so later. His second wife stayed up here for years, long after his death. Then she died, and it was empty for some time. She had no children. She had a niece, I think, who inherited but didn't want it. And now Mr. Sutton has it. I hope he didn't pay too much, that's all. It's going to cost him an arm and a leg getting it habitable again. Getting rid of the ghosts,' he finished, with an empty smile.

There was a burst of birdsong from the nearby trees.

'Are you really going to hear that phony Russian countess?' he said.

'Yes,' she said. 'Like you, I believe in ghosts.'

He shook his head. 'Just shadows,' he said. 'Phantoms.' He took a few steps back towards his mother's grave. 'My brother died in battle,' he said. 'Ypres. July. Nearly six years ago.' He touched the edge of the gravestone. 'I'm just glad she wasn't here to see it.'

He turned away, and she followed him back towards the gate. At the edge of the field he stopped. 'Those are your ghosts,' he said. 'Across the plains of France, of Germany, lie our war-dead in their unmarked graves. "The war to end all wars", but it won't. Your officer class in their London clubs, raising their glasses of champagne in the light of the chandeliers, they can't wait for another war. And meanwhile, Inspector Mothballs is trying to entrap a troubled woman into admitting that she poisoned two people in an English village.' He set off down the track, and she followed him.

They walked in silence until they were out on to the lane once more. They could hear voices ahead, behind a shabby fence.

'You want your story?' he said to her. 'Here's your story.' He pushed at a broken-down gate. She could see a small building behind, a once-pretty wrought-iron structure with broken windows. 'The summerhouse,' he said. 'It belonged to Bertha's family. Bertha's sister used to rest here, in those long months of ill health. Bertha loves this place, and of course, now she's inherited it, but the church is determined to claim it as part of the old graveyard. They say the deeds show it's part of the church land, rather than an adjunct to the Wilkins field on the other side. All this was going on when the elder Miss Wilkins died. That's why it's so neglected.'

She could see police moving about within the tumbledown structure.

'They'll have taken the body away by now,' he said.

They stood side by side for a moment, then he turned away. 'Oh well,' he said. 'You could always ask your Russian countess for clues.'

'There's no need to be insulting,' she said.

He stopped. He met her gaze, and his eyes were dark and anguished.

'Mrs. Christie,' he said. 'If anything – anything at all – could prevent the injustice that I fear, then I too would grasp at it. I love Bertha Wilkins. I've loved her since she first came to the village to take over her sister's house. She has suffered more than anyone can know. She has believed herself to be in love with Cecil, and to be abandoned by him. She has believed herself to be wronged by Miss Banks. But nothing in that woman's heart is capable of murder.' His words ended in a muffled sob. He covered his eyes with his hand, then turned back towards the lane.

They walked, side by side, until they reached the village.

At the crossroads, he offered her his hand. 'Mrs. Christie. Thank you for listening to me,' he said.

'Mr. Fullerton. I am not a detective,' she said. 'I write stories, that's all. Everything you've said to me, you should say to the police. Miss Wilkins needs you,' she said. 'I am going to go home, and immerse myself once more in the fictional world, which has only a thin connection to this one. In the meantime, there is a real murderer out there. And if it is not Miss Wilkins, then the police need to know.'

His eyes were locked with hers. He nodded. 'I shall do as you say. And the séance,' he said. 'Is that part of the fictional world too?' He gave a brief smile. 'Does that, too, have only a thin connection with our world?'

She smiled back. 'I shall no doubt find out,' she said.

Chapter Eight

Agatha poured herself some lukewarm tea and wondered when her husband would be home from the City. The teapot was made of white porcelain, painted with pink roses. The tea tasted stewed. Outside there were darkening clouds, the beginning of a stormy sunset.

She stood up from her desk and wandered to the fireplace. She stared, unseeing, at the Cornish seascape in oils that hung above it.

She wondered, vaguely, why her husband was working such long hours.

She wondered, vaguely, about poison. Belladonna, perhaps. It would work for this story, she thought. The sister's father, perhaps, could be a doctor. He could easily get hold of it.

But in real life? It's not that easy just to poison someone. A woman's weapon, everyone said.

Only Miss Wilkins wanted both Phoebe and Cecil dead. She'd said so herself. But everything Clifford had said seemed to have a ring of truth. No doubt Inspector Mallatratt would find out soon.

A ring at the doorbell made her jump.

She heard Alice open the door, heard Mary's voice.

'Agatha – are you ready?'

The séance. Of course.

'You hadn't forgotten, you silly? Hurry up, I don't want to miss the beginning. Apparently she comes out in a full length mink coat and a cloud of white smoke.'

'I'm all set.' Agatha closed the notebook on her desk. 'I'll get my coat. Though I fear my old mackintosh will look rather shabby in comparison.'

They set off in the clunk-clunking of Mary's Morris Austin along the quiet lanes.

'Isn't it terrible, these murders at the vicarage,' Mary said. 'The vengeance of a lovelorn woman, apparently.'

'No one's been found guilty by law,' Agatha said, more sharply than she meant to.

'Well, no, but it's only a matter of time, by all accounts,' Mary replied, her brisk manner failing to take Agatha's tone into account. 'Mind you, if I was jilted by a young man for another woman, I might feel like killing them both too.'

Agatha was aware of two thoughts. One was that she couldn't imagine Mary either being jilted in the first place, or minding. And the other that Clifford would have his work cut out if he was going to keep Bertha from arrest.

The entrance to the church hall was thronged with people. There were publicity placards outside. 'Madame Litvinoff,' they said, with glamorous images, white-blonde hair, white coat, black curtains, a curl of cigarette smoke.

There was an official and rather hostile man on the door.

'We have tickets,' Mary said, in a loud whisper, and, grabbing Agatha's arm, ushered her into the hall, nodding vague greetings to similarly fierce and be-hatted women as they passed.

The hall seemed to have changed beyond recognition.

Last time Agatha had been here for a local flower festival, and she remembered lacklustre drapes against damp red brick, although the fierce women were all too similar. But now, black velvet swathed every surface of the walls, and there were red curtains across the stage. There was a heavy scent in the air, and the stage glowed with the light from two huge candelabras either side.

The crowd entered, chattered, settled. And then as the central light faded, an expectant hush fell. The curtains opened, and Mme. Litvinoff stood there.

She appeared rather small, almost frail, in a long, old-fashioned black evening dress and a fur stole. Agatha felt rather cheated of the grand opening that Mary had promised.

Mme Litvinoff took a few steps to the front of the stage. 'Welcome,' she said, in a heavy accent, opening her arms towards the audience. 'I am Madame Litvinoff. I am here for you, only for you. You have come to me, because in your hearts there is a thirst. I can quench that thirst. There are people you love for whom you yearn, for a glimpse, a few words. I can speak those words. I am here because I am blessed with a gift. I am here because in my heart I share your yearning, I know your loss, and I can speak with the voice of those you have lost. Welcome.'

A man in some kind of uniform appeared on the stage with a chair, and she sat neatly into it with a ballerina's poise. And then she closed her eyes.

What happened in the next three hours was both remarkable and everyday, it seemed to Agatha. Madame Litvinoff began to speak, and this time her voice was different, lower, rasping even. At times it acquired an odd, level tone. She would utter a name, and her gaze would alight on someone in the audience. 'I have a Randall,' she said. 'I see uniform. You ... Madam, in the blue hat ...'

'Not Randall,' came a tremulous voice from behind Agatha. 'Randolph.'

'Randolph, yes,' Madame Litvinoff said, with an illuminating smile. 'He says, he is at peace. And he sends his love to you. And to ... your dog ... his name begins with M ...'

'Yes.' The voice was breathless. 'Murdoch.'

'A terrier?'

The reply was even shakier. 'Highland Terrier ...'

She nodded, slowly. 'He says, he knows your dog is looking after you.'

The gaze would then shift, scanning the crowd. Another name, or an initial, or an image, then a gasp of recognition from someone in the crowd, followed by words of comfort, sometimes general, occasionally very specific.

'Your great-aunt Hilda says to tell you that the mahogany casket is yours and not your brother's.'

'I knew it,' came a rough voice from the second row. 'My sister-in-law nabbed it before I had sight of it after Aunt Hilda passed away …'

There were descriptions of graveyards, of battlefields, of rolling hills scarlet with poppies.

'I see yellow flowers,' she said, suddenly. 'Daffodils, perhaps. I see a woman, dressed in black.'

Agatha looked up with a start. Mme Litvinoff was staring straight at her, with an intense but strangely absent gaze.

'I feel terrible anger,' the medium was saying, her eyes still fixed on Agatha. 'I see a grave, overgrown with long grass … I see a mother's betrayal …' There was a blink, a small shake of the head, and then the gaze moved on. Another name. Another man in uniform, at peace.

And then it was over. The curtains closed. The applause was muted, either because of politeness, or because the audience was too moved, too tearful, too choked with their own private feelings to do anything more. People crowded the aisles, filed out of the gate. The ladies seemed less fierce, quieter, smaller.

Mary and Agatha drove home in silence along dark country lanes, thinking their own thoughts. Mary was wondering what to do about Pickle at the stables, he'd gone lame last week and he really wasn't well enough to work. She was thinking about prep schools, again, and how she and her husband were ever going to choose the right one for Justin, when everyone said he was so very bright, and such an able sportsman too …

Agatha thought about daffodils, and a woman in black, and an untended grave.

*

Agatha woke up on Saturday with a single thought. It had nothing to do with Inspector Jerome, or with his love for Bunty. It was everything to do with a diminutive woman in a black evening dress and fur stole, and a possibly fake Russian accent. Which was why Agatha found herself, after a hurried breakfast and a few games with Rosalind, walking up the hill in the spring sunshine, away from the village, towards the summerhouse and the graveyard beyond.

The summerhouse had the same uniformed police constable standing guard. 'Morning, Mrs. Christie,' he said.

'Don't they give you any days off?' she asked.

'A big case, this,' he said, with a certain pride. 'Don't usually get the likes of anything like this round here.'

'I can see that,' she said. She looked at the ramshackle building behind him, the cracked panes of glass. She thought about two laughing girls enjoying an evening away from their work. And now only one is still alive …

'Don't let the Inspector tell you what to think, Ma'am,' the constable was saying. 'I'm sure you know what you're doing.'

'But you see …' she began. 'Mine is only a story. Whereas this …' She waved her hand towards the summerhouse.

He gave her a smile, uncomprehending.

She went on her way.

The sun had clouded over by the time she reached the graveyard. She walked amongst the overgrown tombstones, picking her way through tangles of wild flowers. She wondered why she'd never come up here before. Eighteen months they'd been in the village, she and Archie, and it was only now that she'd begun to think about Sunningdale residing in its own story. She read the names on the stones, often repeated, each allowing the genealogy, the family history to unfold of births and deaths, of people rooted in the very soil of the village.

'Wilkins,' she saw. 'Sarah Wilkins,' followed by her dates. So this was Bertha's sister. The older Miss Wilkins, who had owned the summerhouse which was now inherited by Bertha.

She thought of Phoebe, and Cecil.

Perhaps it was coincidence, that the summerhouse was the scene of the latest crime. Perhaps it is a simple tale of a woman scorned.

But, if it were Bertha … she would need access to the vicarage, late on Monday evening. Cecil's poison was administered just before bedtime.

If Bertha Wilkins had been creeping around the vicarage at that time of night, someone would have seen her.

Agatha walked on, passing more stones, their elegies half hidden behind thistles and bindweed tendrils.

'Dympna, Lady Tapton,' she read. 'Wife of Sir Wyndham Tapton,' she saw. 'Much loved, much missed. "Thou hast my heart in thy hands."'

She found herself wondering whether Archie would think to put such a thing on her gravestone, were she to die before him. She shook herself, as if to dismiss such a thought, then studied the next grave.

'Charlotte Tapton,' she read. 'Eric Tapton.' Their dates were exactly the same. They'd lived just over six months.

The long grass twitched in a quickening breeze. The clouds seemed to herald a gathering storm.

She looked down at the twins' grave. It is not a game, she thought. These gravestones, unfolding their stories, their own brief tragedies. And down in the village, two untimely deaths. A grieving family. A young man's life cut short.

Again, she saw the image of the painting, the portrait that Arthur was restoring. She remembered his words, about finding the truth under the veneer, about revealing the artist's true intention.

Whether Inspector Jerome solves the crime or not. Whether Bunty Flowers agrees to marry him. It all felt thin, and false, and trivial, promising false hope, the hope of order in the chaos, of resolution where in real life there's none.

The first drops of rain began to fall. She turned back towards the village.

As she descended the hill, she could hear a commotion. The revving of a motor car, male shouts, a woman's voice. She came down to the main street to see Bertha, held by two policemen, one on each side, gripping an arm each. She was twisting from side to side, objecting loudly.

'I am not a murderess,' she was saying.

A small crowd had gathered. A plump woman in a blue and orange floral hat was standing, arms folded, lips pursed. 'Oh, you can tell a bad 'un,' she said, to no one in particular. 'The sister was the same. Do you know, she had a bill unpaid at the haberdashers for nearly six months once …'

'I did not wish them dead.' Bertha's voice rose above the murmurs of the crowd. The police were dragging her towards a waiting car. Bertha's gaze scanned the crowd, alighted on Agatha. 'Mrs. Christie,' she called out. 'Tell Clifford, please – go to his house. It's the Laurel Cottage, next to the old well … please – ' Agatha heard no more, as Bertha was bundled into the back of the car and driven away.

The crowd drifted apart. Agatha was aware of Inspector Mallatratt standing at her side.

'There'll be gossip for weeks to come,' he said. 'By the way, Mrs. Christie – Atropine.' He tapped the side of his nose. 'That's what the poison was. Now we just have to work out where she got it from.' He gave her a cheery smile. 'You can have that for your book if you like.'

Chapter Nine

The cottage was made of neat red bricks, the white door framed by a newly painted porch, to which clung a straggly clematis.

Clifford opened the door almost as soon as she knocked on it.

'I thought it would be you,' he said.

'Bertha asked me to –'

'I heard.' He gave a heavy sigh. 'The whole village knows by now. Carted away by Constable Camphor and his merry men. She needs medical care, not that.'

He looked fatigued, and drawn, his eyes shadowed, his clothes awry.

'You'd better come in,' he said.

He led her into a small, bright sitting room. They both sat down.

'I've hardly slept,' he said, as if in answer. 'I keep thinking I should have stopped her, I should have realized how near the edge she was ...' His long fingers fidgeted on his lap. 'I've seen it in men, in the chaps, the trenches, you know ... I'd have recognized it ... but a woman ...' He was talking almost to himself.

'The thing is,' Agatha said, and at her tone he looked up, as if surprised she was there. 'The thing is, it makes no sense.'

'Oh, but I'm afraid it does,' he said. 'And it's my fault. I should have been more honest. I care about that woman very deeply. But I have always felt that I'm in no position to offer someone a future.

Some weeks ago, we had a heart-to-heart, Bertha and me, and I said as much to her. And she said something to the effect that a woman in her position was very vulnerable, and that it was for her to decide what counted as a future.

'I don't think I really understood at the time. I knew that she had set her cap at Cecil, she was very keen on him, very keen. And I knew that I wasn't in the frame when it came to her thoughts of the future. But you see…' He leaned forward, and his eyes had a nervous brilliance. 'What I think now, is that she chose someone who would never choose her. She chose to fall in love with the unattainable because she didn't believe herself worthy of being loved. I think she believed that perhaps Cecil was a way out for her, because in some odd way she knew he was in love with Phoebe all along.'

His manner was calm, she realized, and there was something rather studied in his account. In the silence that followed she could hear the grandfather clock in the hall, the clunk of the cogs as the pendulum swung.

'Bertha lost a baby.' Clifford seemed to blurt the words out. 'She'd hate me to tell you, but it is the truth. She was due to marry the man, and he didn't want to marry her. And she was in anguish about what to do, and then the baby died, and so here she is, no husband, no baby. Lost in grief …' He put his hand to his forehead.

Again, Agatha could not shake off the sense of a performance.

'My mother used to talk about that,' he went on, 'when she was in service at the vicarage. This was under the old vicar, of course. The new one doesn't have that kind of money. My mother would talk about the burdens of women's lives, the hasty marriages, the terror of the shame …' He raised his dark eyes to hers. 'If this war has given anyone any kind of hope, surely, it is for a new order, to throw off the shackles that so bind up women's lives …'

He fell silent again.

Another clunk from the clock in the hall.

'Atropine,' Agatha said.

He looked up. His expression was veiled.

'That was the poison,' she went on. 'Whoever administered it had to get it to the vicarage on Monday night.'

He sighed. 'She'd often go to the vicarage. The vicar would chat to her about Our Lady and the Saints, and all that nonsense, he knew she needed help and for some reason all those fairy tales comforted her. She was there that evening.'

'Oh. Are you sure?'

He breathed out wearily. He nodded. 'I drove her there myself.' He raised his eyes to hers. 'And if she wasn't at the vicarage, she'd be at the summerhouse. She told me she'd been there that last evening, when Miss Banks and Miss Holgate had been there, laughing together. She said they'd let her join them. Well, they had to, I suppose, it was hers, after all. But she told me, how lovely it was, she said, to feel normal. To feel like a woman who has friends she can laugh with. That's how she described it.' He fell silent, and Agatha was silent too, each reflecting on their own thoughts.

The rain had stopped. Agatha gathered her coat around her. She got to her feet. He stood too and followed her out to the hall.

'Well,' Agatha said, 'it's all in the hands of the Inspector now. Let's hope that justice is done.'

He reached out and shook her hand in a formal way. 'Thank you for coming to see me, Mrs. Christie,' he said.

*

The lanes had the scent of spring rain and the overhanging branches sparkled in the sunlight.

Agatha wondered why Clifford Fullerton was putting on a show. She had a sense, as she walked back to the village, of a closing-in. If it was a story, she thought, there would be the various sites of places where the drama unfolded, such as the summerhouse, and the graveyard, and now they'd all begin to be brought to bear on a single centre.

It occurred to her that she knew, suddenly, clearly, where that centre was.

Five minutes later, she rang the bell at the vicarage. The door was opened by the maid that Mrs. Ettridge had described as 'continental'.

'I wondered if the curate was in,' Agatha said.

There was a nod, a scuttling away, and then Robert appeared.

'Oh,' he said. 'Mrs. Christie.'

'I thought perhaps we might have a chat,' Agatha said.

He led her into the library. 'If you don't mind,' he said. 'It's quiet in here and the police say we can use it now.'

'I don't mind at all,' she said.

He pulled out a chair for her. It was a well-made oak chair with an upholstered crimson seat. 'Gwendoline is in the church,' he said, 'working in the parish office, and the vicar is currently doing his visits.'

'How is Miss Holgate?'

Robert's features seemed to crumple. He shook his head. 'She barely speaks,' he said. 'I care for her so terribly, but she won't look at me, she won't say anything, if I appear in a room she immediately leaves it ...'

'I'm sorry to hear that,' Agatha said.

'I know it's about Cecil. Whatever he had come to speak to her about, she must have some kind of awareness of what it was. And I didn't help,' he went on. 'I got upset, you see. He said he wanted to tell her something, and she was behaving so strangely, and I put two and two together ... and now she won't speak to me.'

'You don't know what he wanted to tell her?'

Robert shook his head. 'I've no idea. And before he could ... Before he could do anything, that awfulness happened.'

Agatha waited for him to settle on his chair. 'And do you still feel that you are likely to be blamed for these events, as you told me on Tuesday?'

He glanced at her, then looked away. 'I feel terribly responsible,' he said. 'Arthur was saying to me, last night, that I shouldn't blame myself, even though it was me who insisted that Cecil come. But I just keep thinking, if it wasn't for me he might still be alive ...'

'Arthur's right,' Agatha said, gently. 'You can't blame yourself for the way things turn out.'

He gave a brief, sad nod. 'I suppose so,' he said.

She waited a moment, then said, 'It was atropine, the poison.'

She was surprised by his response. He snapped to attention, staring at her intently. 'Atropine?' he echoed. 'It's a whooping cough medicine.'

'How do you know?'

'Cecil … Cecil said he'd brought some for Mrs. Garvey's poor boy. He'd brought it from the clinic, as the doctor here had asked him …' The words faded on his lips.

There was a silence, in which each considered this. Then Agatha said, 'Do you know when the vicar here tried to acquire the old summerhouse?'

His gaze was distant now, as if his thoughts were elsewhere. 'The summerhouse?' He shrugged. 'I've no idea. But Gwen would know, it must be in all those papers she's sorting out.'

'I could ask her –'

Robert held up his hand. 'She's suffered enough.' His voice was full of feeling. 'This was supposed to be a new life for her. This was supposed to be the start of the life she deserves, a life of gentleness and grace, and reading, and improvement.' He looked up at her. 'If you only knew how greatly she's suffered. All those brothers and sisters, that terrible poverty, and then she was sent to some Poor School. She has changed so much. She smiles, she laughs … she

74

reads. Or rather, she used to. She won't come in here now …' His voice cracked.

'Surely …' Agatha began. 'She can find that happiness again?'

Robert's hands twisted in his lap with agitation. 'When Cecil arrived,' he said, 'on Sunday, he mentioned that he'd brought the medicine for the Garveys. And Gwen said she'd take it up there herself. As she was friends with Phoebe and she was going to see her anyway.'

'But –' Agatha tried to calm him. 'The dosage for a small boy with whooping cough – it's not going to be enough to kill a grown man?'

Robert looked at her. 'Cecil said, it's very concentrated. He said that to her. He said he'd write down instructions for how many drops to give…'

'And then where did Miss Holgate go?'

Robert shook his head. 'As far as I know, she went straight to the Garveys to find Phoebe and drop off the medicine.' His gaze fixed on hers. 'And then … on Thursday night, Gwen said she was meeting Phoebe at the summerhouse.'

'And Miss Holgate found the body.'

He fixed her with look of anguish. 'Please don't tell anyone, Mrs. Christie. I'm sure there's another explanation.'

Agatha got to her feet. 'I'm sure there is,' she said. 'But I would like to have a word with Miss Holgate.'

Robert, much subdued, led her out of the vicarage, and along to the side entrance of the church. The door was unlocked. He pushed it open, and then left her there, slipping away before anyone could see him.

Agatha knocked loudly on the open door, then took a step inside.

There was a damp, smoky, candle-wax smell. The lobby was built of rough grey stone. At the end of it was a heavy wooden door, which stood ajar.

'Hello? Miss Holgate?'

Gwendoline Holgate exclaimed with surprise as Agatha appeared in the doorway. The room was high-ceilinged, with a tall, arched window, through which filtered the afternoon sunlight. Miss Holgate was seated at a large mahogany desk, which was piled high with dusty files. Agatha could see other piles stacked around the desk on the worn red carpet.

Miss Holgate looked at her through pale, nervous eyes. She was hunched at the desk, and her thin fingers rested on a pile of papers.

'I'm sorry to intrude,' Agatha began.

The girl shook her head. 'I don't mind, Ma'am,' she said, in a barely audible voice.

'There are some questions to which I'd like the answers,' Agatha said. The girl looked up in horror, but Agatha added, 'Not from you – from all these.' She waved her hand towards the files. The girl's posture softened.

Agatha gazed at her. 'When did you last eat?' she asked her.

'Don't much feel like eating,' Miss Holgate said.

'I'll tell you what.' Agatha spoke briskly. 'I'll go and arrange for us to have some sandwiches, and tea, and then you and I can go through these together.'

*

Much later, Agatha left the vicarage. She had found Gwendoline Holgate to be helpful, and very hardworking. They had pored over files of parish records, deed boxes, births, marriages and deaths. They had settled into companionable silence, with the occasional exclamation, and the passing of a paper from one to the other. They had eaten sandwiches, and drunk tea, and Gwendoline had become pink-cheeked and increasingly forthcoming. They'd chatted about the books in the library, how Gwendoline had been reading novels, 'We'd only ever read the bible at school, I didn't know things could have proper endings…'

Agatha didn't mention the summerhouse, or the atropine. Instead, she asked if she could borrow two of the files, not to mention it to anyone, she'd bring them back in the morning; and Gwendoline, clearly nonplussed, agreed.

'They're not all here,' she said. 'Mr. Fullerton took some of them away last week.'

Agatha considered this. 'You don't know which ones, do you?'

Gwendoline shook her head.

Agatha gathered up the files she was taking. As she did so, Miss Holgate touched her arm. 'I just wish I'd had the chance to talk to Cecil. I don't know what he wanted to tell me,' she said. 'I'll never know. He was a friend. Robert thinks it was more than that, but it wasn't, it really wasn't … And then Phoebe's gone too, and that's another friend.' Her eyes welled with tears. 'The problem is I bring bad luck on people. That's the problem. One of my sisters said that once and I now I think she's right –'

They began to talk out to the main door. 'You musn't think that way, Miss Holgate,' Agatha said. 'Whatever has happened here will be solved. And you can get on with your life. And in any case,' she added, 'Robert cares about you very much.'

Gwendoline looked up at her with tearful eyes.

'Robert needs you as much as you need him,' Agatha said, standing on the church doorstep in the afternoon sunlight. Then she departed, leaving the young woman standing there. The church rose up behind her, and Agatha had, once again, a sense of the history of the village, the stories in the fields beneath, ever deeper, ever more mysterious.

All she knew was that certain questions needed to be answered. And that somehow, she hoped, the answer lay in the two files now tucked under her arm: the deeds of the Wilkins house that showed all the plans of the boundaries of its land; and the register of funerals for the village going back at least fifteen years.

Chapter Ten

'Well, it's bound to be a fake.' Archie twitched the pages of his newspaper. The French windows were open, and cool evening air drifted in from the garden.

Agatha looked up from her notebooks. 'What is?'

'Tutankhamun,' he said. 'This Egyptian king they've found. Everyone's going mad about it.'

'Why a fake?' She smiled at him, but he seemed deadly serious.

'You expect me to believe it's lain there undiscovered all this time, and then this chap goes marching in and finds it all as those savages left it centuries ago?'

'Archie, dear, they were hardly savages.'

'Well, high priests, then. Hieroglyphics. Whatever they were. And they say it's cursed,' he went on. 'Instant death to anyone who crosses the threshold.'

'Now that bit, I'm quite prepared to believe is a fiction,' Agatha said.

He took a sip of his drink, then went back to his paper. The room fell silent again. The dog at Agatha's feet shifted.

Agatha returned to her notebooks. She thought about the Holbein, locked away in the old shed. She thought about Arthur's painstaking steps to prove its veracity, to help the vicar realize its true value. She wondered, briefly, about the church bell, and whether the value of the Holbein would match the costs of the restoration.

'Sunday tomorrow,' Archie said, suddenly. 'Thought I might pop up to London.'

'London?' She looked up. 'But –'

'Just for a couple of hours. Put my nose in at the club.'

'Oh.'

'What about you?'

What about me? she wanted to say. She looked at him, half-hidden behind his newspaper. *What about us having the kind of Sundays that other married couples have, where we take our daughter out, where we pay visits, see my mother, or my sister, or play with our daughter at home, or do the garden, walk the dogs in the meadows…?*

'Any plans?' His gaze had returned to his paper.

'I'm having tea with Mary,' she said.

He nodded, half-hearing. 'The village will be a nightmare,' he said. 'Crawling with police, and reporters, and all sorts of hangers-on. The sooner they prove that woman did it, the better, and then we can all be left in peace.'

Another silence. Peter the dog snuffled at her feet, and Agatha bent to pat him.

The story is taking shape, she thought. *It is centred round the summerhouse, the graveyard. The vicarage. And there is one other place. One other piece of the jigsaw.*

She got to her feet, smoothed her skirt. Alice had gone home, and there were evening tasks, tidying the kitchen, folding sheets, sorting the mending pile. Peter stretched out his front legs then got to his feet too, anticipating bed-time snacks.

Archie turned the page of his newspaper.

Agatha left the room, Peter trotting at her side.

*

My husband was right about one thing, Agatha thought, as she walked past the church on Sunday morning, watching the crowd of hangers on. Undeterred by the morning drizzle, they stood, a gaggle of men in raincoats, stopping passers-by, asking them if they knew the dead man, if they knew anything about that poor murdered girl, if they had ever met the scheming murderess … There was even a photographer, his camera all set up, trying to get an image of the village street, despite the rain and the churchgoers hurrying towards the porch as the bell tolled in its old, cracked way, inviting people to Morning Prayer.

Agatha kept her umbrella low over her face and slipped away from the high street, away from the village and up the lane.

The walls of Hainault Hall seemed even more dejected under the grey sky. She opened the rusty gate and went up the drive.

She noticed the door was ajar, so she pushed at it and found herself in the hallway. She surveyed the staircase with its rough, unpolished wooden steps, the portraits on the wall showing people who once belonged, now forgotten.

'I thought I heard the door.' The voice echoed from above. Then, light feet on the bare staircase, and Arthur appeared.

'I'm sorry – I did ring the bell …'

'Miles away.' He offered her his hand, which was warm and smooth. 'I have to say, I'm glad to see you. Very few friends in this, it turns out. I mean, they do what they can, the village, but in the end I'm rather a stranger in their midst …' He spoke lightly, but his face was drawn, shadowed with sleeplessness. 'And of course, what can I say? I miss Phoebe terribly. All those hopes of the future … if only I'd asked her to marry me. If only I could say, my "fiancée". Then people would understand my loss.' His eyes were red-rimmed, as if from long hours of tearfulness.

'How's the restoration going?' She followed him along the hallway, and he showed her into a wide, light, high-ceilinged room.

'Slowly,' he said. 'The vicar keeps coming to see if we're any further on, but I try to tell him, it's a long haul, restoration. Can't risk spoiling it.'

The room was well-furnished, with chintz armchairs, and occasional tables. And here, too, the family portraits still hung on the walls.

'You've done very little here,' she said. 'It must be as it was left by the previous owner.'

He smiled. 'You mean, I'm living in an old lady's house.' He threw a glance around the room. 'It'll take time to make it my own,' he said.

She paused in front of a portrait. It showed a man in military uniform, a line of medals gleaming on his chest.

'He looks rather appealing,' she said. 'Nice smile.'

'Some of the portraits are good. That one feels like a real likeness,' he said. 'Not that I'd know. It's of Sir Wyndham Tapton, the last in the line.'

'Is his grave up on the moor?'

'Oh no. He died out in India, I gather. He had a grand burial out there.'

There were other portraits, and Agatha was aware of shadowy faces peering down on them her she settled on an armchair.

'Families,' he said, as if reading her thoughts. 'Sometimes I think I got off lightly. There was just me. And my dear mother.'

'No father?'

He shook his head. 'He died when I was young. I never knew him. My mother moved to London to get work. We managed. Everything I am I owe to her hard work.' He sat down opposite her. 'It's good enough for me.' He looked around the room. 'All this history,' he said. 'I can carry it lightly, you see. Because it isn't mine.'

She smiled, but he looked suddenly, terribly sad. 'I was so sure Phoebe would join me here,' he said. 'We would have transformed this place. New life, a new future …' He smoothed his hand across his forehead.

'I have been wondering about the cause of her death,' Agatha said.

He gave a brief, sad, smile. 'Ah. The teller of stories. However … there is no mystery, unfortunately, about poor Phoebe. It seems quite clear that she got the wrong side of the younger Miss Wilkins, and that through some terrible chain of events involving access to poison, she took her revenge.'

'It was atropine,' Agatha said. 'Whooping cough medicine, they say.'

He nodded. 'Mr. Coates brought it himself from London, I gather. Phoebe was so grateful to him, they were all so worried about that little boy. Heaven knows how Miss Wilkins got hold of it. I just wish I'd realized what danger Phoebe was in …' His voice shook with feeling.

Agatha hesitated, then said, 'Mr. Fullerton is convinced she's innocent.'

'Oh, Mrs. Christie, he's bound to say that.' Arthur's voice was thick with emotion. 'I would do exactly the same. The man loves her.' A shaft of sunlight broke through the clouds, catching the edges of the paintings on the walls, glinting against the glass of the cabinets. 'And, as with all men, he probably never told her how much. Until it was too late.' He touched his fingers against his eyes. 'At least Phoebe knew. I console myself with that. That I did at least have the chance to declare my feelings …'

There was a silence. Agatha was aware of pity for this young man, his hopes and dreams cut short. She wondered what it was like to love like that, with such intensity and passion.

He had gathered himself. 'Well,' he said. 'I should get on. The vicar will want to see progress.' He got to his feet. 'Now, that – that's the real mystery in all this,' he said. 'Reverend Collins's need for money. I'm not convinced it's all about the church bell. And between you and me, I fear that Mr. Fullerton has something to do with it all as well.'

She glanced at him. 'You do?'

He gave a brief nod. 'Mr. Fullerton's mother was in service in this house,' he said. 'I'm sure he's told you, it's a fact he's rather keen on. But there's something odd about it all. His mother was very connected to Sir Wyndham, through the charitable trust he founded in his first wife's name. He employed Mrs. Fullerton to work with him. And there seems to have been a dispute, a question of inheritance, to do with the adjoining land, you see. The graveyard is across the way there, and then the Wilkins summerhouse, and I gather that there's some conflict there, some old dispute about boundaries, and promises made and broken …' He sighed. 'As I say, Mrs. Christie, I'm just glad that for me it's all a fresh start.'

She followed him out to the hall. It was dark, after the spaciousness drawing room, but the sun's rays fell from the narrow window above the door. They illumined a painting by the stairwell, a portrait in a thick gold frame. It showed a woman, with a mass of pinned-up hair, dark expressive eyes, a pale, floaty dress, a vase of yellow tulips.

'This one is rather good, isn't it?' Agatha said.

He nodded. 'I think so, yes. The family did know some good painters, clearly.'

'Who is it?'

His face shadowed. 'The wife of Sir Wyndham. His first wife.'

'Lady Tapton? But – she's the one buried up the hill? With her two babies?'

He nodded, visibly moved.

'A sad story,' she said.

He reached up and touched the frame. 'As I say … families.'

'And that painting?' She pointed at the one on the opposite wall. It showed a man and a woman, seated on a sunny lawn, next to a stone statue. They were gazing at each other with an air of devotion.

'The same painter, I think. I don't even know who the couple are, but I like it very much. I like the ironwork of the bench they're on, look …' He touched the edge of the frame.

'Are these valuable, these paintings?' Agatha asked.

He turned back to her. 'I can't trace the painter. If he was known, then maybe. But for all I know, they're worthless.'

'Unlike the Holbein,' Agatha said.

He threw her a look. He hesitated, then said, 'Between you and me … I think it's fake.'

'Is it?'

'It can take a while, with a good fake,' he said. 'But there's something about the inner layers of paint, the brush strokes are too broad for the time, they just don't feel right. And there's an over-paint on the background. It just seems too … recent. I'm doing more tests on it.'

'Oh dear,' Agatha said. 'There goes the new church bell.'

He gave a thin smile. 'I haven't yet mentioned it to him,' he said. 'I don't know how I'm going to tell him, to be honest. His heart rather set on it, y'know.'

'You can trust me,' she said.

His gaze was direct. 'I know,' he said.

She glanced back at the portrait of the couple. It was so romantic, and she wondered how people did that in painting. It was difficult enough in writing, she thought.

As if to echo her thoughts he said, 'It's the problem of the officer class, you see. Trained to keep our feelings in check. And then, when it really matters, when there's the woman with whom we want to share our life, standing there, so beautiful … and we're tongue-tied. So much human suffering could be avoided, it seems to me, if only we men could express what we feel.'

Now if only Inspector Jerome could find it within himself to say something like that, Agatha thought. Instead of pulling up his shabby collar and being tongue-tied. Officer class, she thought, that's the trouble.

'You put it very well,' she said.

'Thank you. At least in my work …' His gaze drifted to the glass doors that led to the studio. 'At least there I can be honest. It's all that is left to me now.'

'I should let you get on,' she said.

'Well,' he said. 'Thank you for coming.'

Agatha walked back down the track. She thought about the painting hanging on the wall, the woman in the pale dress with the vase of flowers. She remembered, suddenly, the words of Mme. Litvinoff: 'Yellow flowers,' she'd said. 'Daffodils … a grave, overgrown with long grass …'

But then Agatha remembered that in the medium's vision, the woman had been dressed in black, not a cream silk evening gown.

The image of Bertha, in her long black dress, stepping through the daffodils, came to Agatha's mind.

Chapter Eleven

'I blame the war,' Mary said, pouring tea into two large pottery cups. 'It's made these young people much too romantic.'

Agatha smiled. 'Do you think so?'

Mary passed her one of the cups. It was roughly glazed and very heavy. 'Cicely insisted I have these. She fired them herself in her new kiln. Terribly proud of them, she is. Not sure I like them, but I didn't want to be rude. Still, the tea tastes the same. You don't take sugar, do you?'

They sat in the sunlight on Mary's veranda. The rain of the morning had given way to a bright afternoon. Rosalind played on Mary's lawn with a large box of brightly coloured bricks.

'I have something to show you,' Agatha said. She bent to her bags and produced the dusty files. She passed one to Mary.

Mary read the ink writing on the label. 'But – these are Parish papers …'

'I've borrowed them,' Agatha said. 'Don't tell a soul.'

'Wouldn't dream of it.' Mary began to leaf through the yellowing papers.

'The old summerhouse …' Agatha began.

'Here it is.' Mary pointed at a thick, foolscap sheet of paper. She peered more closely. 'Of course, you won't remember, it was before your time, but there was a fuss about whether the land belonged to the Hall. It was all muddled up with the Charity that his first wife set up, and the previous vicar was involved with it too. It came to nothing, of course.' She handed the page back to Agatha. 'How odd. It must belong to that poor younger sister now. What else did you find?'

'I found much of interest.' Agatha placed the page carefully back in the file. 'I found that Bertha's sister Sarah died of a fever, two years ago, at the age of thirty-nine. Bertha herself was thirty-two at the time. I also found the baptism records for a baby, that Bertha gave birth to at the end of last year, and which died a week later. She's buried up in the graveyard, near Bertha's sister. They named her Emily. I also found a marriage certificate. Look.' She opened another of the box files and pulled out a paper which she handed to Mary.

'Bertha Wilkins. Married –' Mary stared harder at the page, put her hand over her mouth. She looked up at Agatha. 'Clifford Fullerton? Last August?'

'The pregnancy wouldn't have showed.'

'His baby?'

Agatha took the certificate back. 'I've no idea.'

'Why is it secret?'

'I don't know.'

'I mean,' Mary went on, 'why on earth didn't he tell anyone? Is he ashamed?'

'Or is she ashamed?' Agatha said.

'And if so, what of?' Mary shook her head. 'It's all very exciting. It's just like one of your books, Agatha.'

Agatha gazed out across the lawn. She could see her daughter, her pink dress against the fresh green of the grass, her curls golden in the sunlight. 'Oh Mary,' she said. 'If only it were.'

Mary looked at her friend. After a moment, she said, quietly, 'You mean it's not a game.'

Agatha nodded. 'All this is too real. Two deaths, two tragedies, and so many other people's lives affected too …' The image appeared to her, of Arthur's tearful face. 'Real life, you see, it has no resolution.' She gave a brief smile. 'I rather wish I had Sylvia Ettridge's approach. She seems to think the whole thing is a huge lark. She keeps leaving me notes offering to help with "my investigation" – as if that's what I'm doing. What I want to do, is just go back to my study and get on with my writing.'

'Quite. As you say, it's not a game. However …' Mary placed her cup on the tray. 'There is one similarity between the way you are in your work, and the circumstances in which you find yourself now. Which is, that you believe Bertha did not poison those two unfortunate young people. And that you need to find out who did.'

Agatha gazed at her friend. 'Mary – how do I do that?'

'You behave like one of your detectives.'

'But Inspector Jerome is just plain hopeless –'

'Well another one, then. Imagine a woman more like you. Older, perhaps. But bright as a button. A quiet intelligence – like you, in fact. What would she do?'

Agatha considered this, her head on one side. Then she smiled. 'Mary – you're right. A woman detective. Certainly older than me. And as you say, sharp as anything.'

'She'd stop at nothing. She'd just take action.'

'She would. She'd go straight to Clifford and say, why were you lying?'

'Actually,' Mary looked at Agatha, 'she might not. She might make sure she had all the information she needed first, before she challenged anyone at all.'

They both looked up, as Rosalind ran towards her mother. She was clutching a bunch of daisies, crushed in her tiny fingers, and she handed them to her mother, laughing.

Agatha held her child in her arms, her lips against the soft curls.

'The vicar,' Mary said. 'Start with the vicar. That's what our lady detective would do.'

*

It was some time later when Agatha knocked at the vicarage door. She'd toured Mary's garden, admired the begonias, looked at the new strawberry patch – 'I wouldn't go too near, the whole thing is an ants nest, it turns out...' She'd greeted Ernest, returning from his game of golf, and then taken her leave, returning Rosalind to Sefton at the house.

And now it was evening, and her hand was on the vicarage door.

The door was opened by Reverend Collins.

'Oh. Mrs. Christie.' He stood, unmoving on his doorstep.

'I'm so sorry to bother you,' she began.

'Only just finished Evensong,' he said. 'Hardly any takers either. I blame the weather.' He stood aside, somewhat reluctantly, she felt. 'To what do I owe the pleasure?' he added, also reluctantly.

'Reverend Collins,' she said. 'I'd like to know what exactly connects Clifford Fullerton with Hainault Hall.'

He studied her, standing one step above her, looking down at her. Then, as if weary of it all, he stood aside to let her in.

*

'It's all rather a mess, between you and me.'

Five minutes later they were sitting in his study, on crimson leather chairs. The room was rather narrow and stuffy, and lined with old books.

'It's all about Mr. Fullerton's mother, Moira. A good woman, she was, Mrs. Christie. The ensuing misunderstanding is not to be laid at her door, oh goodness me no …'

'I gather the charitable foundation is concerned with the East End of London.'

He nodded. 'Exactly that, Mrs. Christie. Moira Fullerton worked for Sir Wyndham in the old days of the Hall. She was there when his wife died, and they were both greatly affected by it. After that she helped him set up the Charitable Trust in his wife's name.'

'And why is Mr. Fullerton now so involved?'

The vicar gave a heavy sigh. The light in the room was fading with the evening. 'When Sir Wyndham married again, Mrs. Fullerton was, shall we say, no longer welcome at the Hall. She felt betrayed.

There was talk of a promise having been made to her, because Sir Wyndham was extremely grateful to her.'

'A promise of land?'

He nodded. 'It's my belief that Sir Wyndham sincerely thought that the Wilkins land that abuts the graveyard was his to offer, and that he'd offered it to Mrs. Fullerton, who was herself widowed by then, in gratitude for all her hard work. Also, shall we say, in compensation, as his new wife was less than welcoming to Mrs. Fullerton. Now, in fact, Moira Fullerton was a good-hearted woman, and made very little of all this, so when it turned out that the land belonged to the Misses Wilkins, she seemed unperturbed. But Mr. Fullerton has reawakened this old wound, it seems, in the light of this dreadful business here ...' His gaze travelled to the door, as if sensing the shadows of the library beyond.

'He is convinced that Miss Wilkins is innocent.'

The vicar glanced up at her. He nodded.

'And I have to say,' she went on, 'I rather share his feelings. She doesn't seem like a murderess to me.'

'Where human nature is concerned, we can never tell, Mrs. Christie.'

'And is Mr. Fullerton still involved with the charity?' she asked.

'A little, yes. I'm not quite sure what he does, but it seems he knows the women who run the clinic in the East End there.'

'And it's through him that Robert came here?'

Again, a nod. 'I gather so. Certainly, his godmother, Mrs. Ettridge, put in a word for him, once it was being discussed. But I gather the initial suggestion came from Mr. Fullerton. Robert was working in the Chaplaincy at the hospital there. I have to say, I'm warming to him. He's quiet, Robert, but very hard-working, and sincere in his faith, which is rather rare in the young these days.'

'And he found you Miss Holgate too?'

'The same way, yes. Through the school there, the Providence Chapel school. And again, another very good appointment. Although …' he hesitated. 'It's a question of Parish Funds,' he said.

'Dwindling attendance,' Agatha agreed, feeling slightly awkward.

'I mean, my staff costs are mostly covered. But the fabric of the buildings all need work. And that bell of ours is not going to last much longer. I'd hate it to be silenced. Dear Mr. Sutton has been so very helpful, when he came to me about the Holbein, so very persuasive about it being genuine, it would really solve all our problems if he turned out to be right.' He got to his feet. 'And now, I really must get on.'

She followed him out to the hall. He went to the front door, opened it, peered out into the dusk. 'Another warm evening, Mrs. Christie. Though we could do with the rain. These spring showers don't last.'

He turned to shake her hand, all reluctance gone. 'I have to say, I do tend to agree with you about Miss Wilkins. I was always rather fond of her. She was often here, calling in for a chat. Miss Holgate had become fond of her too. And I know she could be difficult at times, and rather uncontrolled where her feelings were concerned, but I really wasn't sure when those police took her away like that. On the other hand …' His gaze went to the library door. They stood in silence, reflecting on the events of the last few days. He sighed. 'It is all rather a test of one's faith,' he said. He seemed to have changed, as if being a Reverend was just an outer layer which had now fallen away, leaving an ordinary man, full of the doubts of ordinary men.

'We're not used to such things,' Agatha said.

'No,' he said, with feeling. 'We are not used to such things.'

She took a step down the drive.

'Thank you for your visit,' he called after her, with a new warmth.

*

Agatha walked home in the sultry evening, listening to the last chatter of the birds as they quietened for the night.

She felt a tightening sense of anxiety. She had a sense that this story was far from over, that there was still the possibility that there was a murderer at large.

The evening stretched ahead of her. The parish box files awaited, stacked on her desk next to her notebooks. Inspector Jerome would just have to stay as he was, for now.

Chapter Twelve

The rain that the vicar had hoped for duly arrived. On Monday morning, Agatha struggled towards the church, trying to carry box files whilst holding an umbrella above her head.

Miss Holgate opened the church side door. A wave of relief passed across her face,when she saw that Agatha was carrying the files.

'Oh good, I can put them back in their places,' she said, leading Agatha inside. 'Were they any use, Mrs. Christie?'

'Oh yes,' Agatha said, placing them down on the desk with a thump. 'Very useful indeed, Miss Holgate. I have learnt many important things.' Agatha noticed Gwendoline's expression, a tightening, anxious look. 'Although, I would very much like to see the papers that Mr. Fullerton squirreled away. You see, it is quite likely that the papers he took away show that he is, in fact, married to Bertha Wilkins.'

This time Gwendoline didn't try to hide her response, which was wide-eyed shock. She sat down, hard, on the nearest chair. 'Married?'

'He could hide the copy certificates. But he failed to realize that these registers contain the history of all the transactions carried out on Church premises. Even secret ones, at dead of night last August, with only a clerk from the Parish Council and his maidservant as witnesses.'

'Eva?'

'Yes.'

'Before I came here,' Gwendoline said, almost to herself.

Agatha sat down across the desk from her. 'Miss Holgate,' she said. 'Could you explain exactly how you came to be working here?'

'Yes, of course.' Her face was once again smooth, childlike. 'Mr. Fullerton suggested it to the vicar. And because he knew those ladies who worked in the clinic, and you see, they were part of the charity who ran the school, and so when the vicar said that he needed someone, they chose me. And I'm so glad they did,' she finished, with a rush of relief.

'Why did Mr. Fullerton suggest it?'

Gwendoline shrugged. 'I suppose he knew that the vicar was struggling with all this.' She waved her hand across the piles of boxes.

'Did Clifford know you?'

'Oh, no. Not at all. Not until I was put up for this appointment.'

'But he knew Robert.' Agatha was speaking almost to herself. 'And Robert knew Cecil.'

'Cecil? Yes, they'd met, in London, through the charity.' Her face clouded. 'Poor Cecil,' she said. 'Poor Phoebe too …' Her eyes filled with tears. 'We loved that summerhouse,' she said. 'Phoebe and I. We'd taken to going there a lot now it's got warmer. We'd talk about the future, all our hopes, about who we'd marry, we'd laugh and laugh … And sometimes I'd go there on my own, and take some tea and some books, and just read and read, but now … Now I don't want to go there any more.' She dabbed at her eyes with her fingertips.

Agatha broke the silence. 'That night, when you and Phoebe were there – Bertha Wilkins joined you.'

Gwendoline nodded. 'We didn't really want her there, but she was being friendly for once, and anyway it's her summerhouse, and we didn't know what to do. She'd brought sherry. I'd never had sherry before, usually just tea, there's a flask in the vicarage kitchen which I always use … But Bertha had brought sherry, and three glasses, I don't know why. We thought she'd come to throw us out, as it's her house, but she seemed pleased to find us there, she said we were welcome, and that she was sorry if she'd been horrid to Phoebe. And then poured the sherry.'

'And you all drank it?'

A brief smile lit up her face. She shook her head. 'Phoebe said she didn't like it. She'd tried it at her parents' house and she said she was never going to have sherry ever again. So just Bertha and I had the sherry and Phoebe had the tea. It was all a bit odd. Bertha had been hanging around Phoebe for days, at Mrs. Garvey's house too, and I think Phoebe was just relieved that she wasn't being a nuisance for once.'

'Does Miss Wilkins know Mrs. Garvey?'

'Oh, everyone knows everyone in this village,' the girl said.

Agatha leaned back in her chair and surveyed the heaps of files. She turned back to Gwendoline. 'Miss Holgate – there is no other way of putting this, but – you are the last person to have seen Phoebe alive.'

Gwendoline gave a heartfelt sigh. 'I know, Mrs. Christie. The policeman said that to me too. That Inspector, when he questioned me, he said they always talk to the last person to have seen the deceased alive, that's what he called her, the deceased …' Her voice tailed away.

'Is there anything you want to add, anything at all you can think of to tell me?'

Gwendoline fixed Agatha with an intense, wide-eyed look. 'There is one thing, but it's not about Phoebe. It's about Robert. I think the thing that Cecil wanted to tell me was about something from my past, something from the East End. If Robert ever … if he ever gets over all this, and he might … I want to know who I am.'

Agatha looked at her. 'What do you mean?'

'One of my sisters, once, when we were fighting, she said, "It's not as if you're family anyway."' Gwendoline was staring at the table in front of her, her hands clenched in fists.

Agatha's mind was working. 'You – you were adopted?'

Gwendoline looked up at her. 'I don't know. It only happened once, and then Ma gave her a clip round the ear and told her not to talk nonsense, and I never asked. But if Cecil had been working in the East End, he might have seen something or spoken to someone … that's all I can think of, that would make him want to talk to me like that, all urgent like that.'

The room was quiet. Only a rustling coming from the chimneybreast, perhaps mice, or nesting birds.

Agatha spoke again. 'Robert knew Cecil,' she said. 'Would he know what Cecil wanted to tell you?'

Gwendoline shrugged. 'He hasn't come here to see me. Only once. He stood, over there by the door, just standing there, and then he went out again. After that I try not to be alone with him.'

'It seems to me,' Agatha said, getting to her feet, 'that there are now several more people I need to have a chat with.'

*

Agatha's first stop was only a few yards away, at the vicarage. She rang the bell. The door was eventually answered by Eva, as she now knew she was called. Eva was in black with a white apron, on which she was wiping floured hands.

'I wonder if I might have a word with the Curate,' Agatha said.

Robert was in the dining room, polishing silver. He greeted her and pulled out a chair for her.

'They've got you working, haven't they?' she said, smiling at him.

The smile was not returned. He folded his polishing cloth neatly and placed it on the table.

'Mr. Sayer,' she said. 'Do you regret taking this post?'

He looked up then, and gazed at her with a look of misery. 'Oh, Mrs. Christie,' he said. 'I just feel I'd be letting everyone down if I left.' He sat down dejectedly at the table.

The vicarage dining room was a large, spacious room with a polished mahogany table at its centre. It had the feeling of being underused, and Agatha wondered why the poor young man was polishing silver that would probably go straight back into the cabinet, never to be taken out again.

'The vicar doesn't really know what to do with me, since these awful events,' he said. 'And if it wasn't for Mrs. Ettridge, or Auntie Sylvia as she insists I call her, I think he might have sent me back up to London by now.'

'Do you want to leave?'

He met her gaze. 'The one thing that is keeping me here, is Gwendoline. Ever since she came to the vicarage to work here, I've felt … I've felt we were meant to be together.'

'And why can't you declare your feelings, Mr. Sayer?'

He raised his blue eyes to hers, but said nothing.

'Mr. Sayer. When we met, last week, you entreated me to come to Bethnal Green, because you were sure that you would be blamed for the murder of Cecil Coates. And yet the police, having questioned you, have left you alone. Why did you feel so responsible?'

He sat in miserable silence.

'How did you meet Mr. Coates?'

This time he answered. 'At the clinic. I'd been doing chaplaincy work in the hospital there, last year, and he was doing his medical training. We hit it off. And then when I came here, he'd often visit, or I'd go up to London to see him.'

'So, last week, when he came to see you …'

'He was hiding something. He seemed so determined to come. But when he got here, he kept asking after Miss Holgate, and I have to say I did get rather shirty with him. He even asked the vicar when she'd be at work. I wish now I'd been clearer about my intentions towards her, just to shut him up, but I hadn't declared myself to her, and it would have been indecorous to announce it to a friend first.'

'I still don't see why you felt so anxious last week.'

He hesitated, then blurted out, 'It's all to do with Miss Wilkins.'

'Bertha Wilkins?'

He nodded, blushing. 'She was working as a nurse, at the clinic, as you know. And then when her sister died, she came back to the village. But she and Cecil had met by then, and they did carry on some kind of friendship. Well, more than a friendship, I think. I know she was very angry when he started visiting here and then met Miss Banks and became very attached to her instead. But then, when the vicar was telling Auntie Sylvia that he needed a curate, it was Miss Wilkins who insisted it was me. And of course, Auntie Sylvia knew me and was very taken with the idea. That's how she told me it all happened. But why should Miss Wilkins want me here? She's hardly spoken to me since I arrived, apart from just here, in an everyday way.'

'Did the police talk to you?'

He nodded. 'They asked what I'd seen, that kind of thing. They wanted to know about Cecil's bedtime cocoa, had I seen it. Of course I hadn't. I sleep in the little room at the back of the house, at the top. Cecil was in the best bedroom, and in any case he was still in the library when I went to bed.'

'Did you tell the police about your suspicions about how you came to be here?'

He shook his head. 'I thought of it. But it amounts to nothing. Just that when the vicar wanted a curate, Miss Wilkins, who hardly knew me, insisted I come. But I'm sure it was so that Cecil would follow me. And then he died, and I felt I'd been part of a plot ...'

'I see what you mean.' Agatha watched him as he pulled nervously at his ear lobe, under his sandy hair. 'However,' she went on, gently, 'it's not a plot of which you have any part. If I were you, I'd shake off this sense of unworthiness and go and talk to Miss Holgate about your feelings.'

'Oh, but she's never alone. And I've never felt about this about anyone before, and I really don't know what to say.' He looked at her with his earnest blue eyes. 'Once I went in to the office, where she works, but I just stood there, I didn't know what to say, and so in the end I just went out again. I felt so foolish.'

'Mr. Sayer,' she said. 'Nothing is to be gained by remaining silent. Please trust me.'

He looked up at her as she got to her feet.

'And now I must talk to the vicar,' she said.

As she left, she saw he had picked up his cloth. But she thought she noticed a new vigour in his actions, a stronger set to his shoulders, as he returned to his polishing.

*

Agatha knocked on the door of the vicar's study, then pushed it open. He was sitting by the window, staring out at the garden with a vacant expression.

He turned to her with a distant, weary look. 'Oh,' he said, as he saw who it was. 'Mrs. Christie. Did Eva let you in?' He got to his feet, with tired, heavy movements, then almost immediately sat down again.

'Reverend Collins,' she said, approaching the desk. 'I'd like to know why Miss Wilkins and Mr. Fullerton were married in secret last summer.'

There was a sharp intake of breath. He stared at her, open-mouthed. 'Mrs. Christie,' he said, with new indignation. 'I can hardly see that that is of any concern to you.'

'Mr. Collins,' she said. 'Miss Wilkins is about to be accused of a crime of which she is innocent, and therefore, I would assert that it concerns us all.'

'Mrs. Christie. I would expect better from you. As far as Parish matters are concerned, I am perfectly aware that you are an infrequent attender, about which I am prepared to be quite understanding. We live in uncertain times, and it seems to me only natural that people have to follow their own individual path. It is in my view one of the great strengths of the Church of England, that it respects people's own opinions. But barging in here, asking me about an event that was very private and only of interest to those two persons concerned –'

'I have other questions, Reverend,' she said, taking a seat opposite him. 'Specifically, who had access to the kitchen in the vicarage on both Monday night and again on Thursday night.'

'The kitchen?' His face was blank, but then a look of comprehension flickered across it. 'You mean, because poor Cecil was poisoned,' he began. 'Oh dear,' he said. 'Oh dear oh dear ...' His tone of indignation had gone, replaced once more by weariness as the implication of Agatha's question began to dawn on him.

'Well,' he began. 'On Monday evening, Miss Wilkins was here. We were having one of our chats ... and the thing is ... Oh dear,' he said. 'Oh dear oh dear ...' He looked straight at Agatha. 'She insisted on preparing warm drinks for people. Tea for myself and Mr. Sutton, who was working late in the barn. And I distinctly remember her saying, "And Cocoa for our young visitor, Mr. Coates".'

His words settled in the space between them. Agatha breathed, then said, 'And Thursday evening?'

'Miss Wilkins was here. But – but with Mr. Fullerton. Briefly. It was earlier in the day, but Miss Wilkins again spoke of tea, and went into the kitchen. I heard her boiling water, I remember now, the clatter of cups ... And then Mr. Fullerton left, and she left soon afterwards.'

'And then at some point, Miss Holgate went up to the summerhouse?'

He gazed at her. 'That I wouldn't know. I don't interfere in the doings of my staff once their work is done.'

'Reverend Collins. You have been most helpful. But I have to ask you about this secret marriage. I know it seems to you to be prying, but I must impress upon you, it is of the utmost importance, if a miscarriage of justice is to be prevented.'

*

Half an hour later, Agatha was standing, once again, outside the vicarage. The vicar had settled himself at his desk once more, having told her all he knew, he said, which was that Miss Wilkins had found herself in the unfortunate position of bearing a child out of wedlock, and that she had confided this fact in Mr. Fullerton, who had taken pity on her, and agreed to marry her and raise the child as his own. Then, unfortunately, the baby was born very unwell, had had a hasty baptism, and had died within a few days of her birth, and was, indeed, buried up in the old graveyard, near Miss Wilkins' sister. It had left the marriage, therefore, in a rather difficult position, and frankly, he did not blame the couple for preferring to put the whole sorry business behind them.

She had thanked him, and had got up to go, but in the hallway she'd turned to him again.

'Reverend Collins, you have been most helpful. There is one other favour that I would like to ask you. It's on a more light-hearted subject, and one that I hope will be more pleasant for you to carry out. I've been talking to both Miss Holgate and your curate, and I can see how this silence between them is breaking their hearts. I'd like to help reunite them in some way. I know it's just the sort of busy-bodying that we village women are guilty of, but I hope you will forgive me for that. It is well intentioned. And so,' she finished, 'I wonder if you would be kind enough to host a tea party in the next day or so, to cheer everyone up.'

His face had brightened. It was as if life had returned to normal, as if the duties of being the vicar of a country parish were entirely shaped around helping busy-bodying village women host tea parties, and that order had therefore been wonderfully restored.

'Oh, Mrs. Christie, it would be a pleasure,' he said. 'We could even use the garden if this rain keeps off.'

Chapter Thirteen

Agatha's next visit was to Laurel Cottage. The noonday clouds were lifting, and there was sunlight filtering across the clematis.

Clifford opened the door. He looked unkempt and sleepless. 'Ah. It's only you.' He stared at her, as if expecting someone else to appear from behind her.

'Yes,' she said. 'It's only me.'

He shifted to one side, and gestured for her to come inside.

'I hope I'm not intruding,' she said.

'That's what they all say. I've had the police here for days, it feels like. I'm surprised they haven't arrested me as well as Bertha. They tell me all kinds of things that Bertha has said, all sorts of things she claims to have admitted to. And I don't believe a word of it, I think they're just hoping they can provoke me into incriminating her. Well, I refuse to do so.' He had wandered into the sitting room, and now stood in the sunlight in the middle of the room.

'Mr. Fullerton,' she said. 'From what I can gather, Miss Wilkins is in fact your wife.'

His response was one of shock. He sank, slowly, into a chair, as if deflated. His mouth was open, but he said nothing. She sat on the edge of an armchair seat and waited.

After a moment he found his voice. 'Did Arthur tell you?'

'Arthur? No.'

'Good. I'll give him that at least.'

'How does Arthur know?'

He stared at the carpet at his feet. 'He got it out of Bertha. He met her, on one of her days up at the grave. We had a child, do you know that too?'

She nodded.

'You don't miss much, do you, Mrs. Christie.' There was a chill in his tone. 'Arthur began to talk to her, he has an engaging manner, as I'm sure you know, and she confided in him. That's all. She swore him to secrecy, and it seems he has told no one else.'

'Why is the marriage secret?'

He leaned back in his chair with a weary sigh. 'I married Miss Wilkins, last August, because it was the right thing to do. And then the baby died. And so there was no reason for us to be man and wife. She had by that time fallen for Mr. Coates.' He picked at a stray thread on the cushion beside him. 'However,' he went on, 'I had in fact fallen in love with Miss Wilkins. That is my tragedy.' He looked up at her, a flash of rage in his eyes. 'The fact that she has now been accused of murder is her tragedy. And now I suggest you leave. Unless there's anything else you wish to ask me, as it seems to be open season on my private life.'

Agatha got to her feet. 'Mr. Fullerton, I apologise. Like you, I am trying to prevent a miscarriage of justice. But I, too, am a private person, and the last thing I want to do is intrude on anyone else's life. I shall leave now, and I won't bother you again.'

*

Agatha walked back down into the village in the afternoon sunlight. She wondered whether anyone in the village would be speaking to her at the end of all this. She thought about her lady detective, and how it would work much better if she was less like herself, older perhaps, not a young mother, but a spinster. *People expect nosiness of a lady singleton*, she thought. *And I'm not nosy. If I was nosy, I would have put another question to Mr. Fullerton. About whether, through his mother and her involvement with the Tapton Trust, he does in fact have a claim to Hainault Hall. Still, there's at least one person who doesn't mind nosiness.*

*

Sylvia's gate seemed once again to be newly painted, and the window boxes showed perfectly matching rows of pansies. There was the barking of dogs as she rang the bell.

Sylvia opened the door herself. 'Oh, Agatha, what a relief. I've been leaving you messages with your Alice but I'm not convinced she passes them on – there's so much to talk about. Has Miss Wilkins owned up to her dastardly deeds yet?'

'Not yet, but I do hope you can help, Sylvia.'

'I'd be delighted to. Do come in. I was just weeding the rose beds but I'll wash my hands and see if Ethel can make us some tea.'

Sylvia was determined to share her theories with Agatha. 'It's a woman scorned, you see, oldest story there is, I'm surprised you haven't used that in one of your books, well I expect you will soon. The thing is, Mrs. Christie, I've been working it out. All Miss Wilkins had to do was get the poison into their night-time drinks. I

111

wouldn't be surprised if Mr. Fullerton helped her too, you know, I've never trusted that man, I know he helps out at the clinic in Bethnal Green from time to time but compared to his mother, who really was so wonderfully committed to it all, he's really rather a fly-by-night ...'

'And that's why I've come.' Agatha's voice was rather loud in the neat sitting room.

Sylvia blinked at the interruption.

'There seems to be a very strong connection,' Agatha went on, 'between Mr. Fullerton and the Charterhouse Trust, which in turn is connected with the Taptons who used to own Hainault Hall. And I thought, if anyone knows, it will be you.'

Sylvia clasped her hands together on her pleated skirt. 'Well, certainly,' she said. 'I'll tell you what I can. It all goes back to Mr. Fullerton's mother, Moira. I know Mrs. Cohen knew her well, and she does see Mr. Fullerton too from time to time, although rarely, I gather. The view is that he's far less interested in the work than his mother was.'

'There seems to be evidence,' Agatha said, 'that Mr. Fullerton has a claim to the Hall. Through a promise made to his mother.'

Sylvia leaned back in her chair. 'Oh, my dear, that rumour has been around for years, and never proved. My theory is that it's all about Sir Wyndham's ghastly second wife. No one wanted her to have the hall, and so everyone rather hoped that someone else might own it after all. The only person who'd really know would be the niece of that second wife, who inherited it from her aunt and who sold it to Mr. Sutton.'

'Do you know where she is?'

Sylvia was bright-cheeked and animated. 'Oh, I can certainly find out for you. I'll ask old Mrs. Tanner who used to run that funny old shop on the corner, selling colanders and mops and things, she seems to know what becomes of absolutely anyone who has left the village. How exciting. I *knew* there'd be more investigating to do.'

Chapter Fourteen

The Berkshire countryside looked particularly appealing in the pink evening light. Agatha motored smoothly along the country roads, following Mrs. Tanner's directions as conveyed by Mrs. Ettridge, 'She's called Miss Gibb, the niece, Miss Nancy Gibb, Mrs. Tanner has told her to expect you, you simply must tell me everything she says, how fascinating, it's all going to be *such* a story …'

Agatha turned down a tree-lined lane and at last pulled up outside a stone double fronted house with shrubs in ornamental pots either side of a cream painted front door.

Agatha rang the bell.

The door was opened by a middle-aged woman with neat grey hair pinned up in a bun, and a tailored green dress.

'You must be Mrs. Christie,' she said. 'Do come in.'

She showed her into a drawing room, which was airy and tidy, with cream upholstery and green cushions.

'I'd heard we had a famous author living in our county,' she said.

'Hardly famous,' Agatha said.

The woman studied her for a moment, then collected herself. 'I can offer you tea,' she said. 'Or lemonade. I made some earlier.'

'Lemonade would be wonderful,' Agatha said.

'I was so sorry to hear about these goings on in the old village,' Miss Gibb said, once they had settled in the drawing room. 'Of course I never lived there myself, but my aunt was fond of the place when she was in the Hall. Although it got too much for her in the end.'

Agatha sipped her drink, which was sharp and cool. 'This is lovely,' she said.

'It's the squeeze of lime,' Miss Gibb said. 'Makes all the difference.'

'The thing is –' Agatha placed her glass on the tray. 'I've been going through some parish papers. And it seems that there was a dispute about the ownership of Hainault Hall.'

'Do you mean that Fullerton man?'

Agatha nodded.

'Oh, dear, I'm afraid I don't trust that man an inch. When I heard what had happened, the vicarage library of all places, and then the Wilkins summerhouse, I had a nasty feeling he was behind it all. I suppose you've seen those boundary plans?'

Agatha nodded.

'That's the problem. And Mr. Fullerton's mother worked for my aunt, well, not for her, but for my aunt's husband, before he died. Then my aunt, as the second Lady Tapton, acquired the house on his death, and that's how it passed to me as her sole heir. And there was talk that my uncle, as I suppose I must call him, had promised Mrs. Fullerton some kind of inheritance. She was a devoted woman, there's no doubt about that, and she nursed him in his final illness, my aunt always said they couldn't have managed without her. But I have to say, there was nothing, nothing at all for her, when it came to the reading of the will. And I don't think she minded for herself, but perhaps she liked the idea of her boy going up in the world and having some kind of position, some kind of share of an inheritance.

'But how he ever thought he had a claim to the house, I'll never know. And then it all got entangled with the Wilkins estate, with that land around the summerhouse being in dispute, and no one being sure where the line had been drawn, and then the vicar got involved, and I think Mr. Fullerton saw his chance to stake his claim too.'

She took a sip of her drink.

'Of course, for me it all means nothing. That house was always a millstone as far as I was concerned. I have no possible use for it myself. So when Mr. Sutton came along, it was really a great help. An artist, too. The family would have been delighted,' she said. 'Particularly my uncle's first wife. She was very artistic, apparently. Very sensitive. It's my belief Sir Wyndham never really got over her death. He married my aunt so soon after, but they never seemed terribly happy. I think he never really had the love to give my aunt.'

She surveyed Agatha for a moment, as if weighing something up, then spoke again.

'I don't usually say this to people, but you see, my aunt Iris was not a nice woman. A very harsh, cruel woman. My father was her younger brother, and he was, frankly, terrified of her. He was sent away to school when he was eight, and he always said it was relief to be at school because it meant he was out of her way. So to have

116

inherited that house from her was a mixed blessing. It wasn't something I wanted to have much to do with, so Mr. Sutton coming along was a great relief. Although, I must confess I'm somewhat worried about the amount of money it will require in maintenance.'

'And Mr. Fullerton?' Agatha prompted.

She sighed. 'As I say, I don't trust him. I know he was hanging around those Wilkins sisters. I fear that he thought if he got in with them he could at last inherit their land and that way make a claim on the Hall.'

They sipped their drinks in silence for a moment.

'A writer,' Miss Gibb said, suddenly. 'I love to read. I read whatever I can get my hands on. Do you know Freeman Wills Croft? A wonderful writer. And E. C. Bentley …'

A sudden mewing interrupted them.

'Oh, Captain, there you are.' She jumped up and opened the door. A sleek, black cat slinked into the room and jumped up on to the sofa next to her, whence it fixed Agatha with a hard stare.

'I've thought of writing myself,' Nancy was saying. 'Although I'm not sure what I'd write about. Perhaps it helps, having a murder take place in one's own village.'

'Really, it doesn't.' Agatha's tone was emphatic. 'Take my word for it.'

'My own life is rather quiet,' Miss Gibb went on. 'I thought of teaching as a profession, at one point. But I inherited comfortably from my father, which means I don't really need to work. I tend my garden, I lead a tapestry group at the church. I don't need much, you see. That's why that house was such a burden. Long may Mr. Sutton stay there, as far as I'm concerned.'

'I have another question,' Agatha said. 'Those graves, on the hillside there –'

Miss Gibb's face clouded. 'The children's grave? Very sad. But do you know, I never heard my aunt express a single regret about those babies. And they were so small, just a few months. I think about that poor man, my uncle as he became, trying to care for those two babies, only to see them die too. They say it was the same weakness that the mother had, that they'd inherited it. I remember the funeral. Two little white coffins. I'll never forget the expression of triumph on my aunt's face. And her husband, standing there, haunted, it seemed, haunted by the ghosts of those two children, their lives barely started.

'But my aunt didn't shed a tear. Not one. Her husband also didn't cry. It was worse than that. He looked ill. Ill with the grief of it. No wonder the marriage was so unhappy. There was even the rumour of a mistress in those years. I wouldn't be at all surprised. A man like that, he would have been yearning for the love he'd known with his first wife. And he'd never have found it with my aunt.'

'When did he die?' Agatha asked.

She frowned, considering. 'It must have been about four, five years later. It'll be in your parish records, won't it, dear. I think he died of grief. And then my aunt mouldered away in that house for years and years, until she finally went into a home. And then last year she died, and the house came to me. And as I say, it was the last thing I wanted. All that misery. Those two small ghosts ...' Her voice tailed away. 'Well, I expect you need to be going.'

They got to their feet, and she led Agatha out to the hall. Captain trotted at her side.

'I hope I've been some help,' she said.

'You have. Really, Miss Gibb, you've been a great help.'

Miss Gibb opened her front door, peered out into the evening air. Captain suddenly bolted past her and ran out on to the drive. They could see the golden flashes of his eyes in the darkness.

Miss Gibb shook her hand. 'It's very nice to meet you. Next time, do bring me one of your books, won't you. I can add them to my collection.'

*

The next morning, Agatha was on the station platform at nine-forty-one, and caught the nine-forty-three train up to London. From Waterloo she caught a taxi to Bethnal Green and went straight to the Charterhouse Clinic. Mrs. Cohen appeared delighted to see her, in between issuing instructions to a rather terrified young man and introducing her to a dark-haired middle aged woman in an extraordinary patchwork coat. 'My cousin,' she announced, 'another one, I think you met Mrs. Solomon before, this is Miss Samuel ...'

Agatha managed to explain the reason for her visit.

'Mr. Fullerton?' Mrs. Cohen said. 'We see him from time to time. Rarely, I have to say, although the Tapton Trust is still very generous to us. Records? I'm sure we can help. Let me find the Brigadier, he's always the one to ask about such things.'

Five minutes later, Agatha was shown into a tiny room with a slit of a window at ceiling level and beige gloss-painted walls. Two hours after that she emerged, brushing from her sleeves the dust of several piles of boxes that had not been touched for months, if not years.

She ate a sandwich at Waterloo station and caught the train back to Sunningdale. She came out of the station and walked away from the village up the hill, towards Hainault Hall. Anyone seeing her would have remarked on how she seemed tense and anxious, and not her usual composed self at all.

She walked up the drive of the Hall, and rang the bell. She was relieved when a familiar figure opened the door.

'Oh, Mr. Sutton. I'm so glad you're here. I was afraid you'd be at the vicarage. The thing is, I don't know whom else to ask, but I really need your help.'

Arthur took in her pale face, her nervous speech.

'Mrs. Christie – what is the matter? Do come in, come in …'

'I have to be honest, Mr. Sutton. I fear that these murders aren't over.'

'But – surely …'

'I have a terrible sense of premonition,' she went on. 'You might say it's just me being a teller of stories, but I fear there will be another victim. And I know it sounds awfully dramatic, but I feel that we have to step in. You and I. I really couldn't think of anyone else to ask.'

'Mrs. Christie ...' Arthur led her into the hall. 'I wouldn't dream of dismissing your fears in that way. Would you mind joining me in the studio, where I was settled?'

She followed him along the passageway, through the green baize door. The musty corridor opened out into a wide, light-filled room.

'It was the games room, I believe,' he said, indicating the space around them. 'Billiards or something. I've hardly touched it. But with this much light, it suits me well.'

She saw his easel. Next to it were untidy boxes of paint. In one corner there was a butler's sink, an old wooden draining board, covered with jars which were smeared bright with colour.

The walls were pale and peeling. There was a fireplace, above which hung a painting, a landscape, she thought, in muted greys and blues. In one corner there was a painting of a man in military uniform. In another, a vivid portrait of a woman.

Arthur found a chair, dusted it off with a rag. 'Now, Mrs. Christie. Do gather yourself and tell me what this is all about.'

'Oh, Mr. Sutton. Your fears that Clifford Fullerton has a claim to your house have proved right.

Arthur threw her a sharp look. 'Are you sure?'

'As you yourself surmised, it's all tied up with the promise that was made to his mother.'

Arthur stood in the middle of the room. He looked suddenly thoughtful. 'That would explain ...' He looked up at her. 'That would explain why he is so angry with me,' he said. 'How did you find out?'

'I was looking at the parish records. The problem is, he's taken quite a few away with him, according to Miss Holgate.'

'Oh that poor young woman,' Arthur said. 'I knew he'd been bullying her.' He sat down on the stool by his canvas. 'But how would this lead to another murder? Surely, with Miss Wilkins now arrested for the two we've already had …'

'I've been to the Clinic. The one in the East End, that our parish is connected to, through the trust.'

'Mr. Fullerton's mother …'

'Exactly,' Agatha said. 'I know Sylvia believes that it's all thanks to her that Robert got the curate's position here, but the clinic records show that Mr. Fullerton pulled all the strings. And at the same time, Cecil Coates had met Bertha Wilkins at the clinic, when she was working there as a nurse. His friend Robert being the curate was just a pretext, I fear, for Cecil to come and pursue Bertha. Then, he met Phoebe, and decided not to have anything more to do with Bertha. But, at the same time, Mr. Fullerton had arranged for Miss Holgate to get the job at the vicarage too. And we all know that Miss Holgate is absolutely certain that Cecil had some information to impart to her, that also goes back to the Charterhouse Clinic. And it's my view that it's to do with her parentage. I am confiding all this in you, Mr. Sutton, because you understand the artist's mind. And because I trust you.'

Arthur was looking thoughtful. 'But – Mrs. Christie – what has Mr. Fullerton to gain?'

'I think he wants this house. He feels his mother was betrayed by those he calls the land-owning class. He has carefully put things in place to stake his claim. I'm wondering if his connection with Bertha Wilkins wasn't just that the land around the summerhouse does actually belong to Hainault Hall. I think the records that are missing from the Parish office are the ones that prove that either way.

'Anyway, I want to put a stop to it all. I've agreed with the vicar to have a tea party. Tomorrow afternoon. Miss Holgate will be there, and Robert. But I realized, if you were there, Mr. Fullerton will declare himself, as he is so angry with you for occupying a house he considers to be his.' She got to her feet, and paced the studio floor. 'Of course –' She turned to face him – 'I would quite understand if you refused and just allowed these things to take their course. But he is so very angry, and I fear for what might happen now that Miss Wilkins has been arrested. Will you help me, Mr. Sutton?'

He reached out and shook her hand. 'I'd be delighted, Mrs. Christie.'

'I've told everyone three o'clock. At the vicarage. I hope I'm not just being a silly woman.' She had come to rest by his easel. The painting was half-finished, and seemed to be a landscape, almost abstract, in bright, angular brushstrokes of red and yellow.

'There is nothing silly about it at all.' He came and stood beside her. 'Please don't judge me by this. It's not yet finished, and I'm not convinced it's any good. I think I should stick to restoration.'

'And that?' Agatha moved towards the fireplace.

'A modern piece,' he said, indicating the painting. 'It says Newquay. I've no idea who did it. But the Taptons clearly were informed in their collecting.'

'And who is that?' She pointed at the military man.

'It says Colonel Paul Tapton. Some family member,' he said.

'And that?'

'It's named Eleanora.'

She approached the painting of the woman. She had a black bonnet, and at her feet were yellow flowers.

'I don't know who she is,' Arthur said, 'but I like the painting very much.'

'Is there a family resemblance?' Agatha gazed at her.

He shrugged. 'I can't see one,' he said.

She stared for a little longer at the woman. She had a sad, expressive face, standing upright, her dress dark against the brightness of the flowers.

'You've been a great help,' she said to Arthur.

'It's a pleasure.'

'I was worried, what with your sorrow …'

'About Phoebe?' He met her eyes. 'It is always with me.'

'All this worries me.' Agatha spoke quietly. 'That people might think it's just a huge game. When you make things up, like I do, when it's a matter of telling a story –' She gazed up at him. 'You see, in a story, there is always a resolution. It's the opposite of real life. I'm worrying that I'm just running away from the truth of things.'

He looked at her warmly. 'I wouldn't accuse you of that. Just because you're a teller of stories, it doesn't mean you avoid the truth. It's quite clear, Mrs. Christie, that you are working very hard to do what is right. And I'm only too happy to help.' He seemed about to say more, but was silent.

In the hallway they shook hands again. He hesitated, then said, 'I wouldn't be too hard on Clifford Fullerton. Whatever his beliefs about this house, I am convinced that his love for Miss Wilkins is honourable and true. I can't say more, but I would ask you to trust me in this. But I am very happy to join you in your tea party and see what we can do.'

'I appreciate it, Mr. Sutton.'

Agatha left him standing in the wide doorway, his hand raised in a wave.

She walked back down the lane. In her mind she heard once again the words of Mme. Litvinoff, about black bonnets and yellow flowers, and a mother's betrayal.

She thought how Arthur had known all about Clifford's secret marriage but had kept his secret. She remembered how Arthur had sprung to Clifford's defence, to assert that Clifford's love for Miss Wilkins was real and true, and not a pretence at all.

Tomorrow, she thought, we shall all gather in the vicarage. She felt a sense of foreboding; a shiver of trepidation.

Chapter Fifteen

The next morning, Agatha appeared on Mary's doorstep, looking distressed.

'It's a matter of cups,' she said. 'I've talked the poor vicar into having this tea party this afternoon, and now he says he hasn't got enough cups, you'd think the vicar would have loads of the darn things …'

Mary looked at her friend with concern. 'Agatha,' she said, 'come in. You need to sit down.'

'I'm completely out of my depth,' Agatha was saying, as she followed Mary into her house. 'I've ended up thinking that I know better than Inspector Mallatratt and his team of chaps, which is just ridiculous when you think about it. Archie was so concerned last night he made me make a telephone call to the Inspector, and I had to blurt out all the things I was thinking. I felt such a fool hearing it out loud. Archie was quite right, of course, just tell the police and have done with it, then you can stop worrying and get back to your own story. But the problem is the atropine.'

'Atropine?' Mary stared at her, concerned. 'Agatha, do sit down, you're making me nervous, pacing like that.'

'It came via Cecil, from the London clinic. It went, with Gwendoline Holgate, to Mrs. Garvey's. A few drops were given to the boy, who got better.'

'It's because it's May,' Mary said.

Agatha looked at her blankly.

'Whooping cough,' Mary said. 'It disappears in May. If you catch it in June, you cough all year.'

'But then what?' Agatha appeared not to hear, still standing in Mary's sitting room. 'Bertha Wilkins was hanging round at the Garvey's. She was also in the vicarage the night that Cecil was poisoned. And she went up to the summerhouse with tea from the vicarage kitchen the night that Phoebe was poisoned. The inspector went rather quiet when I told him all this on the telephone yesterday but you'd think they'd have worked all this out themselves.

'But the point is, Mr. Fullerton knew the atropine was coming from the London clinic, because he knew Cecil. Mr. Sutton said as much, when we discussed it. And Mr. Fullerton was also at the vicarage when the poison was dispensed. And, as we know, he's the husband of Bertha Wilkins. Anyway, I told all of it to the Inspector on the telephone, but now I can't get out of this tea party at the vicarage. I'm feeling rather foolish. Mr. Sutton went on about the artist's sensibility, which is a nice way of saying it, but the fact it I've just got too caught up in these events, much too caught up ...'

Mary led Agatha to a chair and made her sit down.

'Anyway,' Agatha went on, 'the poor vicar is worried about crockery, as we'll be quite a party, so I wondered whether you could bring a couple of spare cups and plates and things. I was going to ask Sylvia, but I know what she's like, she'd bring out all her best things and then wince whenever anyone so much as lifted a cup to their lips...'

Mary rested a hand on her friend's arm. 'Of course I'll help. But promise me, Agatha, when this tea party is over, you'll just call a halt to all these imaginings and go back to your work.'

Agatha met her eyes. 'Mary, I promise.'

*

At two o clock that afternoon, the vicar went into the parish office.

'Ah,' he said. 'Miss Holgate. Oh dear, oh dear. Chairs, you see. Moving 'em about. I don't suppose you'd be able to give me hand?'

At two twenty, Arthur Sutton appeared from the barn where he'd been working to find Gwendoline struggling to carry a large armchair across the hall.

'Miss Holgate,' he said. 'Dear me, surely the vicar hasn't got you doing that? Let me help you ...'

At two thirty Agatha arrived, to find the drawing room in disarray, stuffed with all sorts of different chairs, none of them matching. Arthur greeted her.

'The vicar is fretting terribly,' he said, with a serious tone. 'I'm not sure this was a good idea. And what makes it worse is that Clifford burst into the barn today where I was working on the Holbein and challenged me. He said, "This is a fake, isn't it?" And the awful thing is I had just concluded the same thing myself. And I was about to agree with him, when he started accusing me of all sorts of nonsense.'

He took Agatha's arm, and his voice was hushed.

'He said I'd brought it with me, that for some reason I left it in the barn and then pretended to find it.'

He let go of Agatha's arm, but his gaze was intense.

'Of course, he's right, it is a fake. I'm almost entirely sure of it now. I've been working on it all morning, and I can just tell, the later over-paint, the size of brush stroke … I'm going to have to tell the vicar at some point.'

'Perhaps you should announce it this afternoon,' she said. 'I've set up this silly tea party for no good reason, and everyone will be waiting for something to happen. You can make your announcement then.'

'Oh dear,' he said. 'The vicar will be so disappointed.'

'At least it means you can go back to your own work,' Agatha said.

He looked at her with a brief smile. 'You and me both,' he said.

They were interrupted by a loud ringing on the bell, followed by the sound of Eva opening the door.

'I hope I'm not early.' They heard Clifford's booming voice, and exchanged anxious glances.

Agatha murmured to Arthur, 'Well. Whether we need it or not, the performance must go on.'

'To our places,' he said. 'Good luck.' He disappeared into the kitchen.

*

At ten to three, the vicar appeared in what looked like a new jacket, certainly freshly pressed, in a rather loud shade of crimson.

Gwendoline Holgate hovered nervously. Robert came out of his study, and immediately went to Gwendoline's side. She gave him a shy smile.

At three on the dot, Sylvia Ettridge rang the doorbell. Gwendoline opened the door, greeted her, showed her into the drawing room.

At twenty past three, Mary arrived – 'Sorry I'm late. I was trying to find cups. Heaven knows where the other one went to, I've just brought this.' She handed Agatha one of Cicely's mugs.

Agatha looked at it, disappointed. 'I'm not sure we'll have enough,' she said.

Sylvia frowned at the cup in Agatha's hand. 'What on earth is that? You should have asked me, dear,' she said to Agatha. 'I'd have got out the Wedgwood specially.'

In the kitchen there was much fussing. Clifford was there, for some reason, being grumpy and clumsy, and frowning at the Cicely cup as he tried to arrange tea cups on a tray, only to have them rearranged by Eva.

Out in the hallway, Robert found Agatha and led her to the corner by the stairs.

'Thank you,' he said. 'I spoke to her. You were quite right. Gwendoline,' he added, as if it needed explanation, although his smile said all there needed to be said. 'And now I must go and help her with the cake.'

Agatha was briefly alone, but then Arthur was at her side. 'Clifford has barely said a civil word to me so far. I'm sure that he's planning to spill the beans about the painting,' he said. 'After this morning …'

Agatha looked up at him. He was looking tense and tired, and she wondered whether she looked as bad. 'This whole idea was a terrible mistake,' she said. 'Let's just get it over with.'

She went back to the kitchen, where the vicar was issuing instructions. 'I've got Eva serving sandwiches in the drawing room,' he said. 'We need someone to put out the cups.'

Sylvia and Mary both appeared. 'A milk jug?' Sylvia was saying. 'You really should have asked me.'

Gradually people drifted into the drawing room. Mary stayed to help Eva in the kitchen. People settled down, there was chatter, a flickering sunlight, a pleasant breeze through the open French windows.

Sylvia was talking to Robert, 'What do you mean, it's Autumn where your mother is, can't they even get their seasons the right way round?'

Agatha noticed that Clifford was deep in discussion with Gwendoline.

A tray of tea appeared, and Mary distributed the cups. Gwendoline got the Cicely mug. Then Clifford moved away, and Robert found himself seated next to Gwendoline. Robert began to talk to Gwendoline, and Agatha watched as a smile began to dawn across her face, and their conversation became animated and full of laughter.

Agatha caught Mary's eye and they both smiled.

'More tea,' Mary said. 'I'll take the cups.'

'I'll help,' Arthur said.

'Just avoiding the inevitable,' Clifford said.

Agatha's heart sank. Arthur looked shaky.

'Arthur has an announcement,' Clifford said.

Arthur glanced at Agatha, then determinedly followed Mary into the kitchen where Eva was pouring tea.

A minute or two later, Eva reappeared with the tray, Arthur behind her, and cups were distributed. Clifford was glowering at Arthur, Arthur trying to avoid his gaze.

'What has Arthur got to tell us?' the vicar asked, smiling benignly.

'It affects you, Vicar,' Clifford said. 'I'm sure he'll tell us shortly. Won't you Mr. Sutton?'

Arthur looked nervously at Agatha. Mary had passed Gwendoline her Cicely cup again.

Agatha suddenly said, 'Oh, it's such a shame that Miss Holgate has to have to that awful thing.' She reached for the cup. 'I'll find you a nicer one,' she said, disappearing into the kitchen. She appeared a moment later with the same cup. 'I'm sorry, this is all there is. Mary only brought the one. And there aren't any other cups to be found.'

'I'm sorry.' Mary's tone was sharp, unable to conceal her irritation. 'I did explain I couldn't find its pair.'

'I really don't mind,' Gwendoline said, sweetly, sipping her tea.

Arthur sat anxiously at Agatha's side, as Clifford started up again. 'Well, Mr. Sutton. We're all here. And we're all waiting to hear about the Holbein.'

'Ah. The Holbein.' The vicar was smiling still. 'Is there news? Have we got a value?'

Arthur gazed around the circle gathered there.

'Such a coup for the village to have a famous artist,' Sylvia was saying quietly to Mary. 'I mean, detective fiction is all very well, but Holbein, that's real art, isn't it?'

Arthur glanced at Robert, who'd reached for another cake, at Gwendoline, who had barely eaten but who was sipping her tea, at Sylvia, whose hand was poised over the sandwiches as she murmured, 'Shall I risk another fish paste?'

Arthur took a deep breath, then said, 'The Holbein might be a fake.'

There was a general murmur of surprise.

Arthur went on, 'I did warn you, Reverend Collins, when I took on the job.'

'Oh, no, no, this won't do at all.' Clifford's voice was loud in the room. 'What I want to know is, why did you, Arthur Sutton, secrete a painting into that barn and then pretend to find it and pretend that you thought it might be a Holbein? Eh? That's what I want to know.'

The vicar was still looking from one to the other, with an expression of benign bewilderment.

Arthur was looking straight at Clifford. 'That's a most ridiculous suggestion.' His voice was level, his expression one of great calm.

'Not ridiculous at all. It's the only explanation. As if we'd have a Holbein in our local church. Why, the church itself is only two hundred years old, and most of it has been rebuilt since then.'

Arthur looked at Clifford. 'I did not know it was a fake. I've only just found out. Just because you're angry with me about the house, you don't need to cast aspersions.'

'The house?' Clifford was wearing an empty smile.

'We all know you think you have a claim to my house,' Arthur said. 'And for all I know you want to have Bertha's house too.'

'Now, that's preposterous.' Clifford had got to his feet.

'Chaps, please –' the vicar intervened. 'Let's not spoil this lovely party that Mrs. Christie has organised. She wanted us all to get over these terrible events …'

Robert squeezed Gwendoline's hand. Gwendoline replaced her empty cup on the table.

Agatha spoke quietly. 'The real problem, Arthur, is that Hainault Hall is not yours.'

There was a shocked silence in the room.

'The deeds never passed to you,' Agatha went on.

The hush was broken by Arthur. 'I am the inheritor of Hainault hall.' His voice was harsh, and his expression suddenly steely. 'My father was Sir Wyndham Tapton. And my mother was his mistress.' Arthur was sitting still, and upright, with a strange calm about him.

There was a gasp in the room.

'All of that is true,' Agatha said. 'But your parents weren't married,' she went on. 'And in any case, you couldn't inherit.'

'I was the only heir –' he began.

'Because,' she was saying, 'the true heirs, were the twins. The offspring of his marriage to Lady Dympna Tapton.'

'They died,' he said. 'Their graves are there for all to see.'

'Those poor babies,' Agatha said. 'Six months old.'

'Exactly,' he said. He was staring directly at her.

'But they did not die.' Agatha met his empty stare.

His gaze seemed to falter.

'They were adopted,' Agatha said. 'As you, Arthur, know very well. When his first, much-loved wife died, Sir Wyndham remarried very quickly. To Iris, whose niece I met yesterday. She's a lovely woman. We had a very interesting conversation.'

Arthur had grown pale.

'She had no good to say of her aunt. And what I learned, from the papers, is that Iris forced her husband to give up the children and to pretend that they'd died. The funeral was fake. As fake as your Holbein.'

Arthur was staring straight ahead, unblinking.

'It seems she didn't want to raise another woman's children. He was most unhappy. His unhappiness drove him into the arms of your mother, Arthur. Eleanora. Who managed as best as she could to raise you on your own, and eventually married a Mr. Sutton, who didn't live that long either. Eventually Sir Wyndham died. His will names only his second wife, Iris. And she left the house to her niece. Who describes it as a millstone. When you came along as a tenant, she was relieved.'

'I'm not a tenant. It's mine –' He was steel-eyed, tight-lipped.

'I realized,' Agatha continued, 'from what she was saying, about having to spend money on the house, about how it was so helpful you living here, that she still believed she owned the house. So I went back to the deeds and it all became clear. Once I realized there was a possibility that the twins had been adopted, I went to the clinic, and sure enough, it had been organised via the Tapton Trust. The old vicar, the predecessor of Reverend Collins here, processed the adoption without realizing who these babies actually were. I imagine that with Iris, Sir Wyndham's second wife, pulling the strings, he didn't dare to ask.'

All this time Gwendoline was looking more and more pale.

Agatha turned to her. 'You, Miss Holgate, are the sole surviving heir of Hainault Hall. Cecil was the other twin. And that's why you were both in terrible danger. From the person who felt they were the wronged party in all this. Cecil, tragically, met his end as a result. And when you were sitting in the summerhouse, the flask of tea destined for you was drunk instead by Phoebe, as Bertha appeared, unannounced, with sherry, which you preferred to drink. It was that sherry which saved your life, Miss Holgate.'

Arthur was staring, glassily, through all this speech, but now he spoke. 'You can't prove any of this,' he said. 'This is your story teller's nonsense, it's got the better of you, your fictional world, you're just making it up –'

'So,' Agatha said, 'the atropine that you put into Cicely's lovely cup?'

Arthur went white.

Gwendoline, too had acquired a ghostly sheen.

136

'It's all right.' Agatha turned to her. 'I swapped the cups. Mary did, in fact, bring both, but we had a little performance, didn't we Mary?'

Mary gave a brief nod, a small smile of pride.

'And the poisoned one is currently outside, with Inspector Mallatratt and his people.'

At that moment the Inspector himself came through the door.

'Arthur Francis Sutton,' he announced, loudly. 'You are hereby under arrest for the murders of Cecil Coates and Phoebe Banks, and for the attempted murder of Gwendoline Holgate.'

Chapter Sixteen

The vicarage drawing room looked upside down and disorderly, as if a storm had blown through it but now calm had been restored.

People blinked in the aftermath. Arthur had been handcuffed and driven away by Inspector Mallatratt and his team. Now everyone sat around looking somehow dishevelled. Even the tea things looked shabby, with sandwich crusts and half-eaten cakes sitting randomly on plates.

Reverend Collins was looking around him as if in someone else's house altogether, as if he'd been displaced from the comfort of his own life and given the life of someone altogether different, someone who lived side by side with murderers. He sat, mopping his brow, gazing from one person to the next.

Robert was attending to Gwendoline, who had fainted. She was sitting up, looking pale but otherwise alert. 'You're all right now,' he murmured to her. 'Perfectly OK. But to think that blackguard might have killed you ...'

Clifford had gone to the French windows and was standing, stock-still, gazing out into the garden.

Mary was holding Cicely's cup, the one remaining one, between both hands and studying it, thoughtfully. Sylvia, tucked away in her corner of the sofa, had reached for one of the remaining sandwiches and was now nibbling on it as if hoping no one would see.

'But –' It was Mary who spoke at last. 'How did Arthur Sutton get everyone here?'

Clifford turned to face the room. 'I blame myself,' he said. 'I didn't realize quite what ...' He breathed and went on, 'You see, he'd found out our secret. Miss Wilkins and I ... we were married last year.'

Mary studied the cup in her lap. Sylvia looked up from her sandwich, blinking at the news, yet another fact of village life of which she was unaware.

'And you see,' Clifford went on, 'Bertha didn't want anyone to know. So when you, Miss Ettridge, mentioned your godson, Arthur made Miss Wilkins insist on Robert coming here, as she was connected to the charitable trust at the time. And that way he knew Cecil would come and stay. And he put forward the name of Miss Holgate, from the Providence school, to help the vicar, which is why I suggested her. He must have gone through the parish papers to know all this, as Mrs. Christie did subsequently. And I supported him. I liked the idea of this young artist taking over the old house, I thought his ideas were good ...' A shadow crossed his face. 'I had no idea it was all fake. Everything. Even the painting,' he added, with an empty smile.

He turned to Agatha. 'I have much to thank you for. My Bertha will be freed, with no stain on her character. And as for the Hall ...' He turned to face the others. 'I never wanted the house. I just wanted justice for my mother. But this is justice enough. And to think that you, Miss Holgate will inherit. It really is very pleasing. I'm sure it

139

will be a relief to the niece too.' He ambled to the nearest seat and sat down as if his thoughts still weighed heavily.

'But –' Sylvia almost put up her hand to ask a question. 'The poison,' she said. 'How did he …?'

Agatha leaned back in her chair. 'I realized that on both occasions the poison was administered, Arthur had been in the vicarage. Bertha had made cocoa for Cecil, but Arthur was in the background then. And it was the same with the tea flask intended for Gwendoline.'

'And how did he get the poison in the first place?' Sylvia asked.

Agatha answered her again. 'We know that Cecil brought it from the London clinic. I think Arthur must have taken it from him at that point, when he arrived, and squirreled some away, enough for a fatal dose. After all, the whooping cough remedy only needed a few drops. Only Cecil would have known that Arthur had taken it, and he wasn't here to tell us.'

Mary gathered up the one remaining cup. 'Poison,' she said, almost to herself. 'It really is just as well I don't like these awful cups.'

Sylvia put down her sandwich and surveyed the room. 'Well,' she said. 'Well, well, well.'

*

Then there was the slow clearing up, with Eva quietly carrying plates, tidying chairs, restoring order. At one point Agatha saw her rest her hand on the vicar's arm, giving him a maternal pat. He smiled, vaguely, up at her.

'Reverend Collins –' Sylvia approached him. 'May I see this so-called Holbein?'

The party trouped into the old barn. Clifford removed the cover from the frame and they stood back and surveyed the half-restored portrait.

There was a silence, broken only by the cooing of the wood pigeons in the roof.

'The sad fact is –' It was Clifford who spoke. 'It's really very good. Even as a fake. The man has talent, there's no doubt about it.'

'Perhaps they offer classes in prison,' Sylvia said, crisply.

The vicar was standing a little way back, with Agatha. He turned to her. 'Greed,' he said. 'A human failing. One of which we are all so easily guilty. This …' He waved his hand towards the painting. 'I so fervently hoped … I allowed all rationality to be overcome with it …' A smile crossed his face. 'I shall write about it for my next sermon.'

*

Later, Agatha and Mary walked home together. Agatha told her how the final thoughts had fallen into place.

'It was when Arthur showed me the paintings in his studio,' she said. 'And there was one of his mother. Eleanora. A small painting, tucked away in the corner of his studio. But of course, he knew it was his mother. It's a lovely portrait. And I stared at it, at those eyes, gazing out of the frame. You see –' She turned to Mary. 'They were so like Arthur's eyes.'

They continued along the lane. Agatha spoke again. 'And the peculiar thing is –' She stopped, turned to her friend. 'It was what Madame Litvinoff said, about the woman in black with the yellow flowers. It turned out she was right all along.'

Chapter Seventeen

Bunty Flowers was standing by the window. She was wearing a blue floral dress, with matching shoes, her hair loosely pinned up. Inspector Jerome, as he entered the room, felt that he had never seen such a beautiful woman in his life. "Will you marry me?" The words formed in his mind, and yet, even now, even though they were alone, he could not bring himself to utter them. It was Bunty herself who turned round, who saw him standing there, his hat clutched between his hands. She smiled at him and said, "Oh. Inspector. Do you have anything to say to me?"

Agatha put down her pen. It was evening. A quiet, spring evening. Even outside it was quiet, as if the village had settled, with relief, into its habitual calm. Late that afternoon, Bertha Wilkins had been released from prison and returned to the village. She had stepped out of the police van into the village square, and ignoring the journalists and onlookers, had scanned the crowds for Clifford. He had stepped forward, and she had run into his arms, and Agatha had heard the passion in her voice as she'd uttered apologies for having treated him so badly, entreaties that they might start afresh. Clifford had taken her hand, gazed into her eyes, assured her that from now on, 'Everything is going to be all right.'

Robert had been inseparable from Gwendoline. They'd left the vicarage together.

'A walk in the sunshine,' he'd said. 'Clear the air, get some colour into those cheeks.'

They'd left, hand-in-hand, walking up towards Hainault Hall. Agatha imagined Gwendoline approaching the drive of the house, taking in the astonishing fact that this house was rightfully hers, and that her adoptive sister, all those years ago, had been speaking the truth.

Agatha returned to her page of writing. There he was, Inspector Jerome, turning his hat between his fingers, wondering what to say to Bunty. Poor Inspector Jerome. What can he possibly want with Dorothea, the mysterious woman in black standing by the gravestone?

No, she thought. *Not Jerome. I will marry him off. Dear Inspector Jerome. He can retire to the countryside with Bunty and they can keep pigs. And then, I shall start my new story. It will be a different detective who meets Dorothea. A woman detective. Older, unmarried. A spinster detective –*

She almost said the words out loud, just as the door opened.

'Ah.' It was Archie who spoke, finding her there. 'I just wondered if you'd like a cup of tea.'

If you enjoyed *Murder Will Out* you might be interested in *Dying To Know* by Alison Joseph, also published by Endeavour Press.

Extract from *Dying To Know* by Alison Joseph

Chapter One
Falling

It is the end of the story.

She imagined him on the beach, pacing out the last moments of his life. She thought about him climbing, somewhere high up, up on the cliffs along the coast. Standing, on the top, gazing out to sea. Breathing. Jumping. Falling. One, two, three seconds. And then you hit the water.

After that...

Water in the lungs, they're saying.

Which means, still breathing. For a while, anyway.

And now, here, washed up, a silent twisted heap in the midst of noise, the wind across the beach, the crackle of police radios, the flap of blue and white tape in the breeze.

'Berenice. What you thinking, Boss?'

She blinked. 'Oh. Mary.' She looked across the shingle that sparkled in the sunlight. 'I was thinking…'

'About death, was it?'

'Do you think he fell by accident? Do you think he jumped?

'Usually it's the high points near Folkestone that wash up this way.'

'But wanting to die…'

'You always ask those questions.'

Berenice gave a brief smile. 'Do we know who he is?'

DS Mary Ashcroft shook her head.

'Someone will have missed him,' Berenice said.

'He's been in the water at least twenty four hours, they reckon,' Mary said. 'He's what, forty odd? Well dressed, at least he was till those crabs fancied a bite of Harris Tweed…'

'No one just disappears these days.' Berenice said. She held out her hands in their blue latex gloves. 'The SOCO gave me these. He said, seeing as I was the investigating officer…'

'Of course you're the investigating officer,' Mary said. 'Detective Inspector Berenice Killick…'

'Look.' Berenice held a see-through plastic envelope up to the light. 'Stuff from his pockets.'

'No ID?' Mary took the envelope.

Berenice shook her head. 'We should get back to HQ.'

'"… whence is it that the sun and planets gravitate towards one another without dense matter between them?"'

'What?'

Mary was peering at the envelope. 'That's what it says here. Writings.'

'You're making it up.'

'I'm not. Look.'

Berenice stared, read the words. 'Clever bloke, then. It's always the brainy ones. Do you remember that poor man in Wetherby? Wrote out a ground-breaking formula for a new TB drug and then blew out his brains?'

'We were still Yorkshire-women then.' Mary turned towards the cars.

'Perhaps we are still.' Berenice fell into step beside her.

'You mean, you can take the girl out of Yorkshire…' Mary smiled.

'Something like that.' The pebbles shifted under their feet. The sea had withdrawn into quiet, distant waves, as if to declare itself incapable of killing.

Further inland, beside the pale ribbon of the Hythe road, stands a haphazard arrangement of concrete buildings, which make up the East Kent Lepton Research Institute. Here, in a swish of automatic doors, Liam Phelps, physicist, walks into the control room.

'Elizabeth. You called?' In the wide, bright room there were banks of screens. At one of them sat a woman, in crisp shirt and trousers, her pale brown hair tied back.

'Where is he?' She looked up from her screen. 'It's not like him to disappear.'

'Murdo? Perhaps he went for one of his walks.'

'He can't have done. Not today. Have you seen this?'

He leaned on the nearest desk, one arm on her chair. She sat, smart, upright and nervous. He stared at the data in front of him. Two lines, one red, one blue. 'Full beam – ' he began to say.

'No, Liam, look. Look at the chart for the last half hour.'

He stared some more. 'But these can't be B-mesons…'

'Exactly. It's the same thing again.'

'The same as yesterday?'

'And the day before,' she said. 'Something weird's going on. That new pattern - these collisions…'

He leaned towards the screen. 'Did you check luminosity – what about charge errors?'

'We've checked. Look.' She pulled up a screen, scrolled down it. 'Everything's clear. We've checked and checked. The results don't make sense.' Her voice was soft, with a trace of an American accent.

Liam looked at her. 'And Murdo's missing.'

'It's too weird. This is his experiment – '

He turned to go. 'We'd better call a meeting about these results. Just us five. And the director. OK?

She reached up and touched his sleeve. 'Liam – what about Murdo? It's not like him to disappear.'

'Maguire? I'll keep trying his mobile,' he said. 'Unless you want to?'

She shook her head. 'No,' she said. 'Not me.'

The screens murmured their gentle beeping, and her gaze travelled back to the graphs in front of her. 'Perhaps we should phone the police,' she said.

'I'm not sure it's part of their brief to worry about changes in the make-up of the universe - '

She gave a thin smile. 'I meant, Murdo.'

'I know,' he said.

'Although I guess they're tired of hearing from us.'

'A broken window is different from a missing man,' he said. 'Even if it was a deliberate attack on this building.'

'Just bored kids.'

'Three nights running? And what about the hate mail?' he said.

'Superstition. Or Sci Fi heads. Anyway, Richard has got security guys at both entrances now.'

He glanced down at her. 'I'll be back,' he said. He turned back to her. 'No one else must know about this. Only the team. Understood?'

She nodded, her gaze fixed on the screen.

She got out her phone, called up his number. Murdo Maguire. Her finger hesitated over the name. She clicked it off. In front of her the red and blue lines lurched upwards, crashed downwards.

DI Berenice Killick splashed water on her face. Her face in the mirror stared back. She ran a finger through her long black hair extensions.

It is my case, she thought. A man washed up on the beach, with no ID but his pockets full of weird writings about gravity. I should be in charge.

Had she imagined it, she wondered. That sneer from the SIO on their return, Detective Chief Inspector Stuart Coles, 'Well, Miss Killick, there's no point asking me where he might have fallen from… of course, a little local knowledge might come in very handy at this point…'

Something about the word 'local'. A tone of voice…

The door creaked open. 'Thought I'd find you here,' Mary said. 'We've had a call from Hythe. Missing person. Physicist, works at the lab there. Murdo Maguire, aged 43, white, grey-haired, blue eyes, not been seen for a couple of days. Not out of character, they said, but they were worried about him. He's got a wife up the coast here.'

'That's our man, isn't it?'

'His car's been found too,' Mary said, 'abandoned on the Hythe Road, right by that old lighthouse there. Looks like he drove there with the intent of climbing that tower.'

'And jumping off?'

Mary shrugged. 'Who knows. Anyway, Stuart said, as we know who it is, you and I can go back on the warehouse raid case for now. He wants us to follow up the number-plate sightings.'

'Doesn't that need local knowledge too?'

Mary looked at her. 'Oh, God.'

'I didn't just imagine it, then?' Berenice sighed. 'Is it the Yorkshire bit he doesn't like? Or the women bit? Like he would prefer it if everyone was Kentish, male and white?'

'You don't regret the move, do you?' Mary glanced at herself in the mirror. She was wearing a neutral navy suit, and bright red shoes.

Berenice shook her head. 'You know my reasons for coming south.' She took a lip-gloss out of her bag. 'Physicist?' she said. 'Explains that stuff in his pocket about matter and thing. Funny the fish didn't eat that too.'

'Nah, too clever for fish.'

Berenice studied her reflection. Mary met her eyes in the mirror. 'You're thinking about Him, aren't you? Talking of reasons for leaving Yorkshire. Like, how would his wife react if some DC turned up on her doorstep in Leeds – '

'I wasn't actually.' Her voice was sharp. 'I was thinking about these extensions? I mean, really honestly, I know you said you liked them but maybe a short Afro is best for a new DI.'

'Berenice, would I lie to you?'

'– Like, I look like I'm doing an Alicia Keys cover on the X Factor–'

'Listen, Boss, I had blonde extensions all last year and I didn't look like white trash, did I?'

'I never said trash.' Berenice turned away from the mirror. 'And as far as "Him" is concerned, drowning's too good for him.'

'You know the physicist's wife didn't report him missing. Weird eh? He'd been gone two days and a night.'

Berenice shrugged. 'As far as I'm concerned, nothing's weird between man and wife. Come on. Let's go and talk to that villain about the warehouse stuff. While we've got time.'

'What do you mean?'

'Well, there's a dead physicist in the fridge. God knows what that's going to do to the universe.'

'What is there in places almost empty of matter, and whence is it that the sun and planets gravitate towards one another without dense matter between them?'

Virginia Maguire sat in the shadows of her cottage, the book on her lap. She ran her finger along the parchment-thick paper.

'Whence is it that nature doth nothing in vain; and whence arises all that order and beauty that we see in the world? What hinders the fixed stars from falling upon one another?'

She tutted loudly, her lips tight with disapproval.

'For if Nature be simple and pretty conformable to herself, causes will operate in the same kind of way with all phenomena, so that the motions of smaller bodies depend upon certain smaller forces, just as the motions of larger bodies are ruled by the greater force of gravity…'

She held the book in her lap. Perhaps I should throw it in the fire, she thought. She looked at the fireplace at her side, its dusty black surfaces, the cold ash in the grate.

And what would he think, my husband, to find I've thrown his precious book into the fire…

She picked it up and read some more.

'*The Imprint of the origin of the universe can, in the right hands, be detected in its ancient chemistry. It is a creation of infinite duration, and yet, the question we must ask is, how did matter become matter? Who, or what, set this universe in motion? It is this that we are working to uncover –* '

'Hah.' She spoke out loud. She turned to the very first page, and ran her finger along the line where her husband had written, in pencil, his own name. 'Murdo Maguire.'

Her finger, roughened through age and hard work, brushed against the words. '*We have the authority of those the oldest and most celebrated philosophers of Greece and Phoenicia, who made a vacuum, and atoms, and the gravity of atoms, the first principles of their philosophy…* ' She slammed the book shut.

The thick window panes let in a dusky daylight which picked out the grain of the wide oak window sills, the faded whitewash on the old stone walls.

There was a knock at the door. She stared at it. Another knock. She got to her feet and went to open the door.

A uniformed policewoman was standing there, with a police officer next to her, a man. He gave his name, Detective Sergeant something or other, but she felt only weariness at the sight of them, standing there on her doorstep.

'Mrs. Maguire?' they said. 'Mrs. Virginia Maguire?'

'Yes,' she said. 'Do come in.' But she knew, as she showed them in, as she went to the kitchen to put on the kettle, she knew as they told her about the body found on the beach, a man, drowned, that the moment she had always dreaded, had thought of as inevitable, had come.

She would show no emotion. Like the quiet hiss of the kettle as it sat on the stove, as she listened to their words, 'body found on the beach... initial identification suggests... we're very sorry, Mrs. Maguire...' her feelings would stay hushed, simmering quietly. There would be no rage. Even when the kettle came to the boil, even when its whistle shrieked through the air around her, she would sit there, quiet and pale, her head on one side, listening politely.

Alone at her desk, Elizabeth Merletti, physicist, sat by her computer. Her gaze was fixed on the screen as she clicked between images. Click: multi-colour lines emanating outwards from the chaos. Click: two lines, one red, one blue, intersecting where the beams collide. Click, a graph, a sharp upward black line. Click: a photo; him, standing, in sunshine, by water, head turned towards her, smiling. The blue of the lake, the blue of his shirt, the sun on his hair, the warmth of his smile...

And now gone.

Beneath her feet, sixty metres under the ground, there is a tunnel of ice-cold nothingness and infinite collidings, its giant, glinting engineering conjuring the figures on to the screen in front of her.

But all she sees is a blue and blonde picture of life itself. Her eyes shine, perhaps with tears.

She murmurs to herself, one word. It sounds like 'cheated'.

Tyres sliding into mud. Engines silenced. The flash of head lights on the black bare branches of the trees. Berenice Killick opened her car door. DS Mary Ashcroft did the same.

They surveyed the scene before them. One ancient white van, one caravan, their wheels mired in mud.

'That's the van all right.' Berenice nodded towards it. Mary took a photo of the number-plate.

Silence. Grey afternoon light, grey of the concrete wall behind the caravan. They knocked on the door.

Still silence. They peered through the windows. There were sleeping bags heaped on the seats, empty beer cans on the table.

Berenice stepped back on to the mud.

'So what's that, then, over the wall there?'

Mary looked at the high concrete, the barbed wire on top. 'That's the lab. The physics place, where they're smashing atoms.'

'So that's where he worked, our drowned man?'

'Secret of the universe in there, Boss. Keeping the whole show turning.'

'Shame it can't stop just long enough for us to find our villain at home - ' She stopped, short. There was a flick of curtain in the window of the caravan. 'There's someone there.'

155

Berenice knocked loudly. 'Or do you want us to break this door down – '

The door swung open. Standing there slouched a girl, in a huge red sweatshirt and tattered leggings.

'Who are you?' Berenice said.

'I'm Lisa.'

'Police,' Berenice said, as Mary flashed a badge.

'Yeah yeah, I know.' The voice had a teenage weariness.

'D I Killick and DS Ashcroft. We're looking for Clem Voake. Is he your dad?'

The girl laughed. 'My dad?' She shook her head. 'Look at me, blad. He's a white man, innit.'

Berenice had her foot in the door. 'My dad's a white man too.'

Lisa eyed her. 'You saying you black like me?'

'That's exactly what I'm saying.'

'Black you may be, but you're gavvers all the same.'

'Do you know where he is, Clem Voake?'

The girl met her eyes. 'Don't know. Don't care.'

Berenice turned to go.

'He's at a funeral,' the girl said.

Berenice turned back. 'Thought you didn't know where he was.'

'Just remembered.'

'Whose funeral?'

She shrugged. 'Dunno. Shall I tell him you called?' She gave an empty laugh.

Berenice faced her. 'Yes,' she said. 'And tell him we'll call again.'

At the car, Berenice handed Mary the keys. She sank into the passenger seat, as the wheels span in the mud before skidding out on the track.

'Did you see those marks on her arms? If we don't get him for the warehouse raid, we can get him for child abuse.'

'Child?'

'I reckon she's about fifteen.'

'Do you think she's related to him?' Mary accelerated onto the main road. The rain had begun again.

'Why else is she there?'

'I can think of many reasons, and none of them good.'

Berenice yawned. 'Gavvers,' she said.

'Makes a change from Filth, I suppose. Or Scum.'

The radio crackled against the to and fro of the windscreen wipers.

Berenice's phone rang, loudly. She answered, listened, then clicked it off.

'Well, well. The drowned physicist. They've stopped the Post Mortem. Called in the Home Office. Bruising to the head. Fractured cheekbone. Suggests he was assaulted before he hit the water.'

'Not suicide...' Mary stared at her.

'Unlawful killing. Maybe.'

'Maybe Stuart'll need us after all.'

Berenice looked at her. 'He might need you...'

Mary sighed, shook her head. 'Far be it from me to deny your radar where that kind of thing is concerned,' she said.

'Good.' Berenice yawned, again, settled back in her seat. She watched the drizzle in the windscreen wipers. She thought about the physicist, his last moments, his fractured cheekbone. A fight of some kind, a scuffle on the tower. The wind, the tide high, the sea... Then falling.

Falling.

'Maybe he was pushed,' Mary said.

Printed in Great Britain
by Amazon